Dragon Shield

Guardians of Chaos 2

C.D. Gorri

Dragon Shield

Guardians of Chaos Book 2
by C.D. Gorri
Edited by BookNookNuts
Copyright 2021, 2022 C.D. Gorri, NJ

To my loyal readers, you are the best! <3
Xoxo,
C.D.

STOP! Before you go, sign up for my newsletter and get the latest on my releases, giveaways, freebies and more:
https://www.cdgorri.com/newsletter

Description

He's the leader of an elite force fighting a supernatural war, she's been under a magic spell that's kept her captive for centuries, can they find peace in each other?

Kingston Baldric is a Diamond Dragon Shifter and the leader of the Guardians of Chaos. Holley Mount is a Witch trapped in the walls of the Guardians' Keep for almost three hundred years. A devoted soldier, Kingston has already paid the ultimate price for duty causing him to seal off his Dragon's heart for good. But can Kingston resist the call of his fated mate?

When the Loyalists murdered his beloved Neela to tip the scales in the war to gain control of all magic, he never thought he would recover. Chaos is Baldric's only release until the day when the Guardian's own Keep reveals a secret room to him alone.

In it, he finds the most beautiful woman he has ever seen trapped inside a spell. Holley's body was imprisoned for centuries, but her mind has been very aware of the beings inhabiting the walls of the Keep during that time. She's learned much about modern life and longs to be freed to take her place in the real world. Especially when the pull of her mate is so strong.

Will Kingston accept her after the Fates had already dealt him the harshest of blows? Can Holley keep her freedom without him?

Guardians of Chaos Pledge

I am the watcher in the storm.
I am the iron shield.
I protect against those who seek to control the wild
nature of magic.
I am the guardian of chaos.
To thrive, we must be free.
From chaos comes creation.

Prologue

2oo years ago...

The cold, gray walls of the dark rectangular room seemed far too close for comfort as Holley slowly blinked into consciousness. Her head pounded. Pain reverberated throughout her entire body.

How did she come to find herself in this place? Memories tried to break through her bruised mind, but they were foggy. She heard voices whispering around her, but they stopped as her eyes gradually opened.

"What is happening? Where am I?"

"Quiet, heathen spawn," someone hissed followed by a vicious slap to her face.

Holly gasped at the explosion of pain in her

cheek. Frightened did not begin to describe how she felt. It was dark, too dark for her to see. But then a light came, a torch, she thought and squinted against the sudden onslaught to her sensitive eyes.

"Ah, the Witch awakens?"

Holley stilled at the sound of the one voice guaranteed to terrify her. It could not be, but it was. Preacher Milton hovered over her with a lantern held high. The glow from the candle was bright, hot too, as he held it close to her face. But that was not why she trembled.

It was his angry pale eyes that glared at her from beneath the darkened hood of his cloak. The man who'd hit her was sneering beside him. There was something off about his color and his movements.

His other followers stayed back so she could not make out their faces. A shame, she thought, she would love to have names to go with the hexes she was determined to rain down on their foolish heads.

The townspeople hated her and for no real reason. They did not know her. Never took the time. But why would they? She was half savage in their eyes.

Tainted. Unclean. Holley had heard it all. She'd learned not to care, to be unaffected by the stares of those too arrogant to ask questions and too ignorant to listen to the answers.

The fact she was a Witch only made matters worse. Of course, she did not advertise her powers. That would not be wise at all. Granny Rose taught her better than that.

Oh no. Granny.

"Why am I here? Where is Grandmother?"

"Your grandmother has been hanged for your crimes," he spat, "and since the fires could not take you, Devil-worshipper, this shall be your prison till you die of starvation or the air runs out!"

He opened his arms wide and multiple lanterns along the walls flared to life, manned by his followers. Holley struggled to sit up, horrified when she realized she couldn't.

"You brought me here? To the forest Keep?" she asked, shocked at the preacher's gall.

This place was ancient and sacred to her father's people. Though her dealings with the Lenape tribe were few and far between, she knew the stories. Heard of the strange supernatural beings that had built this place many hundreds of years before Europeans had come to live on this side of the world.

The Keep had been built long ago by a secret

order of Witches and other creatures. Or at least that was what she'd been told.

Holley played on the grounds surrounding the enormous stone structure when she was a child. She'd visited the castle with her Granny Rose to meet with her paternal grandfather. Traditionally, Lenape children went to the mother's tribe, but because her mother was a settler, Holley had been all but shunned.

Only her Grandfather Katonah had agreed to meet with the half-European child to see if she possessed the magic of his line. That had been a cold and eye-opening lesson for young Holley.

Grandfather Katonah had met with her seven times after that day. He'd explained in stunted terms about the magic of their people, and Holley had listened. The old man had died some years ago now, but Granny Rose made sure she did not forget his lessons.

Holley had been doubly blessed, *or cursed* depending on how you looked at it, with magic on both sides. Granny Rose did not possess any particular magical talents, but her mother had. She'd spent her own childhood listening and learning how to make salves, healing balms, potions and the like.

Two very different traditions and customs, but both told the story of who she was.

Holley Mount. Native. Witch. Settler. But she was more than that. Holley was a granddaughter and she had loved her Granny Rose with all her heart. Sadness filled her chest and she sobbed quietly for a moment.

Enough child, it's not the time to be lost in memories, a familiar voice whispered to her.

Holley shook her head. Granny was right. She needed to find a way out of this situation. Her eyes scanned the room, but aside from Preacher Milton who was giving orders to his men who seemed to smear paint or was that blood on the walls, there was nothing of any use.

Beaten and chained to a stone slab deep in the belly of the castle in the pine barrens, Holley was truly trapped. Terror eked its way up her spine. That this place would now be her tomb became quite clear. She struggled against her bonds, but to no avail.

"You cannot escape," Milton smiled wickedly in her direction then nodded at his hooded brethren.

"They're writing a spell!"

"Yes," he hissed and lifted a quill as if he were toasting her.

Preached Milton finished a symbol with a flourish of his wrist, "Do you recognize this cast? No? Oh well, still, I thought an eagle feather suited the occasion," he waved the quill still dripping fresh blood and she winced as droplets hit her face.

Holley suddenly felt as if she'd fallen through ice on a lake and was submerged in some freezing, dark depths she could not see. Her teeth chattered, the cold painful to her, and she screamed her agony.

"The searing pain you feel would be the blood connection you now have with this spell, but you should know that Witch," Milton spat the words at her as if they too could harm.

But what they did was reveal a very terrible truth. The blood they used to cast their magic was hers. Blood magic was the darkest of all arts, Holley knew this and struggled harder against her chains.

"I have harmed no one! You are supposed to be a priest!"

"Your very existence is a harm. You are an abomination and since you will not confess-"

"Confess what? I cannot change my circumstance of birth," she pleaded, but the hatred in his eyes chilled her to the marrow.

"Can't you? Pity. Then you will die here."

Holley closed her eyes and pleaded her case to

the great Creator. During one of her grandfather's visits, she'd learned how her ancestors spoke to their kin through the veil between life and death. he'd taught her how to access that plane.

Pity she never practiced. Relying instead on her healing skills to put food on their table. Poor Granny Rose was gone now, and Holley would follow her into the void. But she was not ready. Not yet.

Life was strenuous within the settlement of Puritans who hated the likes of her. Holley was shunned and treated as an outcast for her tanned skin and black hair. They had tried to tell her that her Puritan mother had been raped by a savage and died in childbirth as punishment for not taking her own life before she could bring her daughter into the world.

She understood it was all lies. Granny Rose and her grandfather had taught her that. She even suspected why Preacher Milton hated her so. Though it did not make this any easier.

"You cannot kill me because my mother did not love you," she screamed as the cold began to seep inside her very bones.

"She should have killed herself before you were born! Devil's whore!"

"My mother loved my father."

"He was a dirty savage!"

"No. He was a young warrior. Descended from shamans. They loved each other, and I come from that love."

"He was a rapist and she a whore!"

"You are wrong Preacher Milton," she defied the man who had frightened her ever since she was a little girl.

"Your soul shall burn for this!"

His blotchy skin turned beet red in his fury. But what had she to lose? He had killed her grandmother, turned the town against her, and was now set on killing her in this place. The very same castle she used to dream about living in as a child.

"Look at me, Demon spawn," Milton hissed as he drew back his hand.

Holley ignored the stinging on her cheek after he delivered one final blow. She glared at him with hardened eyes. Anger was not an unknown emotion for her. She knew it all too well. Had felt it for the likes of the preacher and those small-minded members of the settlement they'd begun miles away in *New Ark*.

Times were changing. Talk of revolution and breaking away from England were all the rage. Holley was a fan of this search for freedom.

Although, she doubted those men had the same ideas about it as she.

She was tired of being told she couldn't do things because she was a woman, a half-breed, a Witch even. They feared her, cursed her name, and as such Milton was able to slander her to where her murder would go unquestioned. She would never understand how people who'd left their country to find freedom could be so unforgiving of those who differed from them.

Her heart squeezed with regret as her body trembled violently from the chill. Puffs of white formed from her breath, and she felt tears rolling down the sides of her face. So cold. So dark. Fear threatened to control her mind, but no, she fought against it.

"Struggle if you will, but I have finally found a way to purge your soul of the evil that inhabits it. My men have traced the images in your heathen books here for you to gaze at until you can see no more. True, you survived my attempts at burning you, and drowning the Devil from your blood, but here you will remain within these walls until you are only a memory!"

"No! No!" she screamed as the hooded cowards began to fill the gaping hole in the wall with brick and mortar.

Holley was going to die. Milton was right. Her wrists ached where the manacles cut into her skin. She'd been beaten and bloodied, starved, burned, and drowned, and finally chained like an animal only to be buried alive behind brick.

She did as he said she would and stared at the runes on the walls inscribed with her blood, wondering at the stupidity of men not for the first time. Closing her eyes to the numbness that had settled over her, Holley knew she did not have long. She chanted the words Granny Rose had taught her.

She could trace their ancestry back to the Lancaster Witches of England. She had magic in her veins on both sides. Power pulsed through her blood and she used that and the words she remembered to tap into the spirits of the Keep. The *manetuwak*.

Hear my call. Answer my need, great manetuwak.

The room warmed and pulsed as the power that resided therein seemed to take a liking to her.

Please, spirits of the Keep. I need your help.

She sensed them listening and wondered for a moment at their origin. Magic in and of itself was neither bad nor good. It was how it was used that determined its affinity.

As if it knew her doubts, the *manetuwak* began

filling her head with information. Yes, it was built as she'd imagined, by *supernaturals*. The Keep was for an order known as the Guardians of Chaos. It was created with the intention of aiding and protecting all magic. Yes, it was a positive force, but remained empty as the New World had been overrun by *normals* far too soon for it to be used for its rightful purpose.

Abandoned to the piney woods that surrounded it, the Keep had noticed Holley when she and her grandmother had come across its lands.

Yes, she answered, *we took many walks through your woods to collect herbs under the light of the full moon and I fell in love with this castle and built fairy-tales in my head around it.*

The collecting of herbs was of course, just another mark against her and Granny. The locals called them Witches and had tried and found them guilty.

Holley had been hanged, drowned, and burned at the stake. She survived all three attempts at ending her life. Granny was not so lucky, she shuddered once more at the loss.

Please, I beg you, do not let them murder me. Protect my flesh, and keep my soul tied to thee, oh keeper of my body. Until the time comes when it is safe for me to awaken. Let me see through your walls and hollows, allow me the freedom to take space and shelter inside your heart, great manetuwak. Keep me safe, keep me hidden, as I will, so mote it be.

Holley felt her own magic rise and swell with each statement and every entreaty. She'd never tapped into quite so much, afraid of the consequences. Above all magic required balance, but this was necessary.

Her mind raced forward for a moment, it was lit up like the sun, then plunged into darkness. The pain went away. Her bruises and cuts healed as far as she could tell. Holley saw a miracle of stars and swirling clouds and mists. She heard a steady hum fill the spaces around her.

There was not one being there with her, but she felt the *manetuwak's* presence and knew she was cared for.

Incredible, she thought as peace began to fill her.

The preacher might have imprisoned her here to die, but she would not perish. She would survive and one day she would walk the forests once more under the light of the moon. Holley would taste fresh air again, she swore it.

Even as she felt her human body freeze and grow still beneath the power of her entreaty, the spell of the *manetuwak* or the spirits of the Keep kept her mind focused and awake.

Until the moment when it was safe for her to awaken, Holley's body would remain frozen in time within the very walls Preacher Milton used to try to kill her.

She was part of the great stone construct now.

Of course, Holley had no idea then that it would take nearly three-hundred years for that time to arrive, but each day she used her magic to try and reach the one man with the power to free her. The one man she had never expected to appear.

Her mate.

Chapter One

"*It's time. You must move on,*" Neela's voice called out to him through the veil.

He stood there for hours, days, sometimes weeks inside his dreams, waiting to catch a glimpse of his fallen mate.

Kingston Baldric could only visit that metaphysical place where the realm of the undead met reality in that precarious state between sleep and wake. It was there that he sometimes caught a glimpse of Neela, his fallen mate.

As time went on, her image began to fade. The vibrant blonde she-Dragon he had known in life was nothing but a pale shadow now. Was he responsible for that too? He could only wonder.

Their connection was less than it had ever been.

The call to move on was too strong for even her fiery spirit. He was helpless to stop it, and yet, he still came to this place seeking forgiveness for sins of the past.

The vows he made were over, but how could he let go? His heart grew tight and his Dragon hissed. The great beast did not like it there. He hated being so close to death. It was something any near-immortal creature would naturally find repulsive.

"I can't. I can't let go."

"You must," she whispered.

"Why must I? Without you, I am alone, Neela. So very alone."

"You must be strong, Kingston. I am so sorry, so very sorry," her whispers grew more and more faint with every word.

He tried to reach for her, but the veil slapped at his still-living soul. It was powerful, as it should be. That barrier would not allow any being with ties to the physical realm entry. Not even a mighty Diamond Dragon. Kingston growled deep in his throat but stopped when he could no longer make out the silhouette of his mate.

"Neela! Don't go!"

"I have to go. It is time. I am sorry for everything. So sorry..."

"I don't care about that now. It was never important."

"I am sorry," her whispered voice continued to diminish, "so sorry. Be happy, Kingston, be loved."

"Neela! No! No! Noooo!"

Kingston Baldric, Diamond Dragon, Alpha and team leader of the Guardians of Chaos stationed at the Keep in the Pine Barrens of New Jersey, woke with a start. Sweat beaded his brow and soaked through his sheets.

His room was unnaturally warm, almost stifling. He tossed off the covers and sat on the edge of the large mattress. He ran his hands over his face roughly, wiping away all traces of that torturous dream.

Fuck. He'd been to see Neela, or *her ghost*, as she was now beyond the physical realm. It was not the first time he'd visited his mate in his dreams, but something told Baldric it was the last time.

His heart squeezed desperately inside of his chest. She'd been taken from him far too soon and there was simply no right way to deal with the loss of one so worthy and deserving of all his best.

Neela had not been a Guardian of Chaos. She'd spoken no vows and had no place in battle. The precious female should have been off limits in this endless war the Loyalists had been waging against the supernatural world.

The Guardians did what Guardians do, they protected magic in an effort to preserve it for all *supernaturals*. They were not like the army or the police. That bit was left up to the Enforcers. If the Loyalists wanted to simply fight, they should have gone after them.

Only, they didn't. Now, Neela was dead. His enemies had decided she was fair game and the rare she-Dragon was targeted.

She'd died far sooner than she should have and with more pain than she'd deserved. He could still hear her crying out his name as she succumbed to her wounds that fateful day. Bloodied and left for dead on the side of the road, it appeared an accident to locals. But he knew better.

Even worse, he was responsible for her suffering and her death. No matter how many wrongs he righted, Kingston would never forgive himself. He would never forget that he was the reason she died so tragically.

All his promises were for naught. Images of his brother, Edgar, raced through his mind. They'd been inseparable once. Since they were young Dragonlings, the brothers shared everything they had.

Secrets, toys, games, books, and as they grew older, even women.

When they met Neela, things changed. The lovely Sapphire Dragon was beautiful with her blonde hair and sparkling blue eyes. She'd captivated both brothers and they'd happily dueled for her affections. Edgar won Neela's splendid heart, but Kingston had delivered the mating mark. Now she was gone and the pain was too much. For a hundred years, they lived together as mates, and now he must learn to be alone.

Shame washed over Kingston as he recalled their last argument. Their relationship was complicated to say the least. He was a private man and could not share this with any of his Guardians, but he knew the secrets he kept would be the death of him someday if he did not learn to let go. Even in death, Neela was still smarter than him.

The sound of her pleading voice echoed in his brain, his refusal, followed by her resolution to find happiness within her life. He never held it against her even as he abstained, but it hurt him to think that she was on her way to meet her lover when she'd been killed.

Of course, he told the others she'd been going shopping. He might not have saved her in the end, but he could preserve her reputation at the very least.

With her soul firmly on the other side of the veil, Kingston had to wonder if she was right.

Was it time for him to forgive himself and move on?

Doubt began to rear its ugly head, but his inner Dragon hissed at the debilitating fucker. Kingston had too much on his plate to start giving in to weakness of any kind.

He needed to be strong for his Guardians. Good leaders could not breakdown in the middle of a war. And that was what this was.

Offner had succeeded in killing Neels, kidnapping Fergie, and overall, pissing him the fuck off. But it wouldn't be long before he met the evil Warlock again. Then Kingston would truly make him pay.

Magic was not the Warlock's personal plaything. He'd destroyed the reputation of the Loyalists, but there were still those who believed heavily in the fundamentals of their credo. Mainly to be dicks.

"Where are you with the search?" he spoke into his cell phone and waited while Elena updated him on what she'd found out.

"There are several warehouses that have

reported suspicious spikes in magical use over the past week in Newark, Kearny, and Harrison."

"Get over there and investigate. Take Byram with you," he told the Panther Shifter.

Kingston rarely used his Alpha voice when giving orders to his Guardians. He preferred to trust in their loyalty and respect for him and their mission. After all, they'd all taken the vow. Each one of them chose this life. For better or worse.

He checked the time. Four hours. That was about all the sleep he got just lately. His dragon puffed out a smoky breath in annoyance. The enormous beast would have liked to snuggle up for a week or two, but he had no time for that. The hunt was on, and it was only a matter of time before Offner was captured.

Meanwhile...

"I need the location damn you," spat the aged Warlock.

"Master, we have not been able to locate the files. If you would just let us try to get the female-"

"We tried that already," he slammed his gnarled hands onto the stained table and pointed at the long scar on his cheek, "see what that blasted dragon left me with last time? No, I will not take the risk of kidnapping the redhead again. Just find me the map she located the first time," he commanded.

His blood pumped sluggishly through his veins. Too much time had gone between his last feeding and a Warlock was only as good as the powers he drained from his last victim. The pitiful Witch he'd happened upon was weak and old, which was why he felt as poorly as this.

Time was running out. The Demon who owned his soul would be coming for him soon and if he could not satisfy the beast with a supply of magic, he was as good as gone.

It must be done now. He had to find that vein of magic deep within the lands. He'd almost forgotten its existence, but he knew it was somewhere. He just had to find it first!

Failure was not an option. After he settled his account with the Demon, he would make the Guardians pay and magic would be his to rule!

Chapter Two

"What the fuck are you talking about?" Furio shook his pony-tailed head at his best-friend and fellow Guardian.

"I am telling you, I am not *just* using my Shifter abilities, *cump*. Check it," Storm demonstrated by holding his right hand high and balling it into a fist.

Black, smoky tendrils began to wrap around his hand almost immediately, and when he threw the punch he'd been winding up, his fist sent that power to the far wall where it shattered as if it were sheetrock instead of the huge eighteen-inch-thick cement bricks.

All of the walls inside the Keep were constructed of the thick, stone blocks. The building itself seemed to take offense at the attack. Immediately following the display, the room grew colder and darker.

No sooner had Storm turned around to smile over his supposed victory at Furio, then one of the broken shards seemed to zoom across the room to smack him in the forehead.

"Ow!" Storm rubbed his head and flung the shard onto the floor.

"Awe, *cumpy*, you fucked up."

Seconds later, every bit of the broken remnants of brick and plaster floated upwards and off the floor. The air hummed and buzzed with energy as the pieces wove themselves back together seamlessly, creating the appearance of never having been broken.

"Sorry, Keep," said Fergie McAndrews in a sing-song voice.

She walked into the room at just the right moment as she always did. Catching her Wolf Shifter mate's glowing blue eyes with a mischievous smile on her lips.

The redhead wore her latest pair of spindly-heeled torture devices, these in an alarmingly bright shade of purple, and headed directly into Storm's open arms. She greeted him with a kiss that was far too personal to conduct in mixed company, but they were Shifters. PDA's were kinda the norm.

Their story was legendary, even if it only began months ago. The love they shared for one another was almost tangible. It hurt to watch, but Kingston remained unmoving and observed the byplay.

He turned his head out of respect once their lips touched, noting with passing interest how the room seemed to warm and glow around the mated couple. It was as if the Keep wanted to bask the lovers in a protective bubble. Odd, he mused. Then again, he'd started to notice something off with the Keep after Fergie had pointed it out over dinner one night.

There was something very different just lately about the place he'd called home for the last few decades. A certain awareness he had not recognized before.

As their group leader and a rare Diamond Dragon Shifter, Kingston was one of the oldest supernatural creatures in the order. The Guardians of Chaos was a well-respected organization, but their numbers were small. He'd been a sworn member for a century. His Dragon hissed as his mind threatened to wander back to the days of his youth.

Don't go there. Not now.

The past was in the past. Best to think of other

things. Like hunting for the bastards who'd attacked Neela, then Fergie. The Loyalist problem was getting entirely out of hand. If they refused to accept that mates were off limits then why should the Guardians have to adhere to the rules set forth by the Assembly?

Kingston was in a seriously pissed off mood. That seemed to be his baseline just lately. But what did he expect with little to no rest? A Dragon needed to sleep, but he was anxious. Unsettled. As if he could sense something big was coming.

But what? Fuck if he knew. Kingston was many things, but a clairvoyant he was not. Besides, it was no use. How could he sleep knowing Neela was gone and it was all his fault?

Grrrr. The Dragon inside of him snarled. The beast's claws scratched against his skin, but it was too risky. He could not let the anger inside devour what precious little was left of his humanity.

And just lately, it felt all too little. His fire was burning low, the heat that flamed his soul was going out. Fading. That happened when mates died, but his was no usual mating. He frowned and rubbed his chest.

It could not be that. After all, when he'd woken up that morning he'd been hotter than a furnace.

"Kingston? You alright, *cump*?" Furio knocked on the wall, his inquiry barely making a dent, "you're growling, dude, like loudly," he added, eyebrows raised high on his pronounced forehead.

The Stallion Shifter was unique in Kingston's experience, and he valued him as a member of the team. He silenced his growl and gave the man a curt nod before exiting to his study.

Sometimes he needed to be alone. Now was one of them.

The wall sconces lit themselves as soon as he entered, as did the fireplace. His computer turned on, but the lamp next to it stayed dark. He frowned deeply, pulling his chair out before sitting his colossal frame down.

He waited, but nothing happened. *Hmmph.* He'd gotten used to the Keep taking care of all the little odds and ends he and his team were simply too busy to worry about. Very odd, he mused, the lamp remained off until he bent forward and tugged the little chain.

"You angry with me?" he asked aloud, shaking his head and releasing a long, slow breath.

He was developing Fergie's fancy for talking to inanimate objects. Fucking hell. Kingston ignored his momentary lapse of sanity and logged in to the

Guardians network to read the latest reports and necessary assignments.

He never thought New Jersey would be such a hotspot for paranormal activity, and yet, here he was leading one of the busiest groups of Guardians this side of the Atlantic.

Even more amazing were these new confounded machines that were equipped with special, magicked software that protected them against all matters of malware supernatural and not.

Kingston answered his correspondences, updated the proper channels on their hunt for Loyalists in their sector, and took a look at the quarterly reports. He felt like a fucking businessman and that was something both he and his Dragon loathed.

A chiming bell alerted him to an incoming message and Kingston switched tabs to his email. His finger stalled as he rolled the cursor over the new message. It was from the Assembly regarding their meeting over Neela Baldric's death.

"Fuck," he inhaled deeply and clicked on it.

His eyes closed as he read their findings. *Murder. Deliberate. Collateral damage in the war against the Loyalists. Tragic. Apologies.*

"Fucking bastards!"

Kingston stood abruptly, overturning his desk

and sending everything on it flying across the room. His Dragon snarled and snapped. Pain lashed at him from the inside out as he balled his fists and took a swing at the wall sending shards of stone flying.

Fuck. He was losing it, he thought as he sank to the floor. The room remained quiet. The stone stayed broken. And Kingston closed his eyes and tried to calm his raging beast.

The door swung opened and Furio and Storm ran inside, halting when they saw he was alone, but enraged.

Smart. Very smart. Kingston was looking for a fight and right then anyone would do. But instead of hurting the very team he was responsible for, he headed for the window.

White diamond-shaped scales began to pop out over his skin and he felt himself losing control over his Shift. And why not? This was a pretty big fucking deal.

With an enormous roar, Kingston tore through the window, breaking glass and brick as his almost seven-foot-tall, two-hundred-fifty pound frame changed into that of a fifty-foot-long four-thousand pound Diamond Dragon. The last of his kind.

Sorrow unlike any he'd ever felt welled up inside him as he shot enormous streaks of flames into the sky and flapped his enormous wings. He opened his jaws and screeched a mournful cry that echoed through the forest.

So much pain, so much anger, he needed to fly. To soar among the clouds to try and forget his sorrows. His Dragon was hurting. With scales that appeared white to the naked eye, but upon closer inspection they were in fact clear and crystal-like, he used them to hide himself from the *normals*.

When he wanted to be seen he could take on any color in the rainbow. It all depended on where one stood when they saw him. And what mood he was in for that matter. His Dragon preened at the thought. He was a tad conceited that way, but there were not many who could reflect any number of hues.

Cloaked from the humans, he flew for what seemed like hours, employing his own special brand of magic to do so. Diamond Dragons used their powers and their special scales to turn themselves completely translucent, and therefore, invisible to the eye.

It was the only way he could hide himself from modern technology. Right then hiding was the last thing on his mind. He wanted to burn down whole cities and sink the earth in fire and brimstone. To make the world suffer as he suffered.

Neela.

Fuck, he was furiously angry. With himself. With the Loyalists. With Offner. And with the Assembly, those bastards.

Collateral damage? Fuck them. She was a precious female. Too few female Dragons had ever been birthed and Neela was cherished in her lifetime.

How could they dismiss her death so easily? How could they expect him to stand down and not search for her murderers? But that had been the last line of the missive.

You will forward all your investigative research into this matter to Home Office where our own agents will collect and study your research and launch an investigation. You have been cleared of all charges.

Cleared of all charges. Him.

Well, they might have cleared him, but Kingston would never clear himself. And he would never give up the search.

Chapter Three

Blood poured from the wound on his lip, but Kingston continued to fight his way to the front line. They'd received a tip through a CI of Byram's that the Loyalists had holed up in an abandoned factory in downtown Newark to regroup.

After Elena had scouted the place in her sleek Panther form, they headed in. A dozen and a half of the fuckers were nestled inside. Like the rats, he thought with a snarl.

Petty and cruel, the bastards hurled potion bottles full of bits of wire, nails, and glass with nasty little stinging spells inside that activated the objects when released. Like a supernatural dirty bomb.

After the Guardians had almost killed their leader for kidnapping and torturing Storm's mate, the group had been wreaking havoc any way they could.

The man, Offner, had been unveiled as a Warlock and as a result, the Loyalists had lost any credible standing they'd had within the supernatural community. No one knowingly backed a soulless oath-breaker.

The Guardians finally denounced them for what they were. Liars and perverters of all that magic stood for.

Byram fought on his left and Furio on his right while Elena engaged their enemies from behind. He'd only taken three of his Guardians with him on this trip to investigate Byram's lead.

The Vampire was inhumanly strong and wicked fast. Elena's prowess and stealth were her finest assets, where Furio's lied in his loyalty. Kingston was honored to have them on his team.

True, he was a fierce Diamond Dragon, but he knew he needed them to win this fight. This war was a long one and required more than speed and strength. It needed endurance, presence of mind, and comrades in arms. The Guardians of Chaos always worked in groups, and this was why.

Still, Kingston felt pretty fucking unstoppable at the moment. Truth was, he'd been feeling off balance lately. Neela's loss compounded with the Assembly's acquittal of his own fault in her death had left him raw and angry.

He'd done his best by the female, but apparently that wasn't good enough. No one knew that more than he.

"Your reign is at an end, Guardian!"

Kingston's head turned just as a green-skinned Gila Shifter leapt into his path. His Dragon snarled furiously in his mind's eye. The fuckers were like cockroaches to his magnificent beast.

"That's where you are mistaken, lizard lips," he reached out with lightning fast hands and had the fucker off his feet and dangling in the air in a split second, "Guardians of Chaos do not rule over anything. We are the keepers of freedom. You are the ones who want to decide who gets to use how much magic, what, when, and where. But that is not up to you."

Kingston growled and punched the Shifter, dropping his unconscious body to the dirty ground before spinning to meet the next attack. The hall was smoky and the scent of waste, human and Shifter, disease, decay, and rot were damn near overwhelming.

"Fuck, they have smoke spells, King," grunted Furio as he delivered a back kick to the head of one

Bull Shifter who'd decided to try a half-Shift in the middle of the fight but only managed to make his head swell up like a fucking balloon.

That's what happened to assholes who didn't respect magic. Shifters were a special kind of supernatural who shared their souls with an animal spirit and could access said spirit through a magical bond that was both sacred and unique.

Maintaining a half-Shift was something only a Shifter with a strong connection to his or her animal and who had exceptional control could pull off. Fuckwit here did not fall into the category.

Obviously, snorted his Dragon.

He rolled his eyes and made a mental note to steer clear of Fergie, Storm's mate, for a few days. His beast was starting to sound like her. Next thing he knew, the damn animal would start fawning over footwear.

Not fucking likely, growled the beast.

A rapid succession of pops sounded and next thing he knew, the halls were covered in a thick, black fog that nearly choked him. Kingston smashed his fist through a wall. They had at least six bagged and tied, but the rest of the Loyalists were as good as gone.

Afterwards, he made a call to have the prisoners

picked up by the local Enforcers unit where they would be tried and jailed for their crimes in supernatural court.

That part of the job was not his concern, and for that Kingston was grateful. He preferred the hunt and the fighting aspect as opposed to the law and order part of it all.

"You ready?" Furio's eyes were bright red, and he was still rubbing them.

"Yeah, stop that or you'll make it worse," Kingston nodded at the Stallion Shifter.

"Fuck, man, it burns."

He snorted. Yeah, it fucking burned. It always did.. He was more than ready to head back to the Keep. Away from the putrid stink and crowded streets of one of New Jersey's most densely populated cities, he preferred the stone walls of the haunted old manse any day.

"Let's go," he said.

Hours later.

Kingston laid his head back against the enormous claw-foot tub and closed his weary eyes. The water was hot and clear, the way he preferred. None of those pesky bath salts that dried out his Dragon's scales and had him smelling like Furio's fruity fucking head of hair.

The fucking Draft Horse Stallion loved his thick locks to be shiny and well-conditioned on any given day, whereas Kingston couldn't give two fucks about hair. His or anyone else's.

Well. That was not exactly true. There was a woman, *his dream woman*, and he meant that literally as in a woman who appeared in his dreams from time to time. She had the most gorgeous hair he had ever seen.

Thick, straight, and impossibly dark. His dreams about her were vivid, especially where her wealth of hair was concerned. It fascinated him. The way it seemed to hang down her back and across her shoulders, like a velvet curtain running all the way past her waist and hips.

He'd often imagined wrapping it around his hand and lifting it to his face. Wanted to feel the strands slip through his fingers. He wanted more than that of course. To know the lady. To get a whiff of her scent. To kiss her plump, wide lips.

Would she welcome him? Her mossy green eyes appeared curious in his dreams. He felt her desire, her desperation, and it pained him to not be able to help.

For some reason, he associated the raven-haired vixen with wildflowers and herbs. Could picture her in a garden where they grew in glorious disarray. Yes, even thinking of her seemed to conjure images of long hair and swirling skirts, laughing faces while she tended a patch of earth that very much resembled the old kitchen garden he must've walked past a time or a hundred over the years.

Of course, it was grossly overgrown with weeds and the years of neglect shone in its rusted fence and barren patches. He felt a sudden pang of sadness in his chest.

No, that wouldn't do. He made a mental note to tell one of the Guardians to have it cleared and tended. Not that Kingston had the sudden urge to go gardening, but for some reason or other, he needed that small garden cleaned out and made ready.

Maybe Fergie would have some use for it. Or perhaps her friend would. The little kitchen Witch was always hanging out at the Keep now that Fergie had permanently moved in.

Exhaling slowly, Kingston relaxed every aching muscle he had in the steaming hot water. Having already washed the blood and muck from the earlier battle off his skin, this was the Dragon's reward.

He would never admit it aloud, but he was hoping to catch a glimpse of the lovely maiden who haunted his dreams. Of course, those dreams were typically followed by overwhelming feelings of disloyalty to Neela, but he would deal with that later.

Right then, he needed *her*. Needed the dark-haired beauty with the curious eyes and fearless smile.

Yes, he thought, *please. Come to me, little one, comfort me. Make me forget.*

His eyes drifted shut and he felt her all around him. Her presence so real he gasped even as he recognized she was just an illusion, a made-up fantasy.

Still, he welcomed the faraway sound of her voice as she crooned. He felt her touch as she brushed ghostly fingertips across his brow followed by a tender kiss so soft it was like butterfly wings on his lips.

Sleep now, my Dragon. Rest, the time is coming upon us.

Her voice seemed to whisper inside of his brain and his beast rose inside of him. Growling softly, wanting to fully awaken, but she hushed and calmed his Dragon like no one ever had before. The silly beast wanted her as if she were real, but she was not. Sad as that fact was, it was still the truth. Someone knocked on the door to his private bathroom and he opened one golden eye and growled softly.

Fucking hell, what now, he wondered.

"Uh, Kingston?" Fergie's voice rang through the door and he sighed as he made to get out of his bath.

He could not ignore one of his Guardian's mates. It would not do for a man in his position. Not in the least.

"One moment," he said and quickly dried off and tugged on a pair of jeans and a clean Henley, "yes?"

He pulled the door open and stared in shock at her appearance. The woman was usually dressed impeccably, in designer heels and smart business attire. She was now, with an added addition.

"Um," he was at a loss.

Kingston had never seen Fergie covered in dust from head to toe. She appeared guilty and her new she-Wolf whined loudly so that his Alpha powers picked up on her obvious distress.

"What is going on?"

"Well, you see," she cleared her throat, "Jessenia and I were looking around in the basement, um, exploring really-"

"You wanted faster access to the internet, didn't you?" he narrowed his eyes aware of the current arguments over WIFI speeds within the Keep.

"Okay fine, I admit it. Hudson's room has the worst connection and I thought if I ran an ethernet cable from the router straight to his room I could plug it in to my PC when I'm home and get my work done faster-"

"How is that coming?"

"Work? It's fine," she tucked her dust-covered red-hair behind her ears with her fingers and tried to remain dignified despite her ridiculous appearance, "anyway, the wall we drilled into kind of um, collapsed, and well, I think you need to see this."

"Should I call Furio? He is the best carpenter among us."

"Just come on. Hurry."

Kingston followed barefoot behind the former normal. After she mated Storm, Fergie's animal soul had been awakened and she was now every bit a Wolf Shifter. Still, he wondered how the hell she stood on those things she called shoes.

They looked downright painful to him, and seemed to defy all laws of physics, but she swore by them. Storm also seemed quite taken with the lethal footwear, judging by the way he showered her with new additions to her collection every month or so.

Whatever. Kingston had no interest in the Wolf

Shifters' shoe fetish. He simply followed where she led, down to the depths of the basement of the Keep.

"I used a power drill to make the hole, I mean I thought half an inch was no biggie," Fergie continued her explanation, but he was beyond listening for the moment.

Something was happening to him. His Dragon scratched and snarled inside of him. The walls seemed to close in the deeper he went into the belly of the Keep, and yet, Kingston could not stop himself from investigating further.

Something was there. Something beckoning his Dragon forward. Magic sizzled along his skin, making the hair on his arms and neck stand up. The air hummed and vibrated with power. Perhaps she'd hit some kind of magical vein or ley line?

It was no secret that rivers of supernatural energy and magic dwelled beneath the earth in what were called magical veins or ley lines. Magic was finite. It was recycled and reused, passed down from one person to the next. Inherited, not made.

He could not be sure just what the female had uncovered, but his beast was hissing wildly and his pulse was racing like mad. He inched forward and noted the distinct drop in temperature. It was downright freezing there.

Jessenia was staring through the gaping hole in the old brick wall. He could tell from her stance that the tiny kitchen Witch was in a state of absolute shock.

"Fergie, take your friend aside," he commanded but refrained from using his Alpha voice on the woman.

He had no wish to start a quarrel with Storm, and the way he saw it she was his Guardian's *conpar*, his fated mate, not a Guardian herself. Therefore, she was not his to command.

Kingston did try to remember his manners when speaking to the woman. Storm was a good man and an even better Wolf. He hated to admit it, but he felt nothing but respect, with perhaps a tinge of envy over the man's good fortune in finding his fated mate.

Yes, he'd been carrying the weight of Neela's death with him for a while now, but it started long before that. He'd tried so hard to honor both the female and his brother, but he had failed them both miserably.

Not your fault, he thought he heard the she-Dragon's voice whisper in his head.

Every single inch of Kingston seemed to stand at attention as he stepped over the rubble, careful not to impale his bare feet on the sharp stone as he entered the small hidden room. His Dragon snarled at the myriad of magic coming at him from every direction. Symbols lined the walls, he sniffed and scowled fiercely. That spell was old, but they had cast it in blood and for obvious, nefarious purposes.

There were too many people there for him to get a good read. Too much noise. Then everything fell away from him as he caught the faint scent of flowers and blueberries on the air.

Grrr. Mine.

He wondered at the thought, but the truth struck him hard. It was the most wonderful fragrance he'd ever smelled.

His eyes landed on the vast slab of winter stone in the center of the small rectangular space. Chest heaving, Kingston put one foot in front of the other and approached the altar.

Yes. Something inside of him seemed to recognize it for what it was. He hated the thing on sight. The stone table was meant to be a coffin, he realized and growled once more.

As his bare feet drew nearer to it, he realized someone was chained to the cold, hard rock. Just like a sacrifice. Kingston sucked in a breath and more of the blueberry flower fragrance invaded his senses. The air was musty and cold, dust motes filled his vision. He waved them away, squinting and calling upon his Dragon's eyesight. The beast had night-vision and as Kingston adjusted to it, he could not believe his eyes.

It was her. The woman from his dreams.

Thick black hair so long it hung off the sides of the altar surrounded her perfect face. She had tawny skin with earthy undertones of golds and coppers, though he could imagine her rounded cheeks with a hint of blush on them. As it was, the cold kept her unnaturally pale. Still, she was, in a word, lovely.

Her wide mouth was slack as if in sleep, but Kingston knew better. He could tell by the furrow of her eyebrows that she was doing anything but rest. Beads of sweat dotted her forehead as she battled with whatever was holding her down and that was when he sprang into action.

Using his Dragon's strength, Kingston gripped the heavy metal chains that were attached to the manacles binding her wrists. He noted with muted fury the bruises that marked the area, a telltale sign of her struggles.

He didn't know who she was or who put her there, but by the gods themselves, he would see them pay! Anger warred with the singular intent to free her inside of him, the latter won out thankfully, and he stretched and pulled the bespelled metal, oblivious to the conversation going on around him.

"Kingston!" someone yelled and he spared them a brief glance as his Dragon hissed at them for their interruption.

He needed the woman freed. Now.

No, not the woman, his Dragon growled, *my woman.*

"Kingston," Storm touched his shoulder.

Kingston turned his head and growled at the Guardian, one word escaped his lips.

"Mine."

"Oh fuck," Storm said and tackled his mate to the ground.

"Hudson," she groaned, but he knew the Wolf would not harm his mate.

He barely spared them a glance. Good thing the Wolf Shifter had such good instincts, he'd known before Kingston what he was about to do. With one well-aimed roar his flames covered the chains, weakening them to the point where he was able to twist the wretched things to pieces.

The metal bits clanged loudly as they hit the hard floor, but he couldn't have cared any less. Whoever had chained this woman was going to die, even if he had to scour the Earth for the bastard!

He rubbed her wrists and hands hoping to bring warmth to her ice-cold body. She was freed from the awful constraints, but still the small woman's eyes were firmly closed. Her face looked pale and in pain. His beast roared inside of him. Carefully, slowly, he leaned down to her face with his hands outstretched but not quite touching.

"Wake up," he whispered.

Her skin began to glow then, and he was helpless save to watch as she struggled with whatever magic held her captive. Golden eyes darted from person to person in the room. Somehow, all of the Guardians under his care had arrived without him noticing.

"Egros," he summoned the one male Witch in the room even though his Dragon wholeheartedly objected to the male's presence, but Kingston pushed his jealousy aside.

He needed to help her and Egros was the one person there he trusted to have the knowledge necessary to do that. The Witch approached and Kingston's lip furled into a low threatening growl which had the man lowering his gaze and baring his throat to him.

His position as Alpha commanded as much and he was grateful Egros did so without hesitation. The last thing he wanted was to hurt the unmated male for coming near the woman.

Mate, his Dragon supplied.

Holy fuck. He had a mate. A fated mate. The idea was simply too huge for him to wrap his draconian head around. Better to take it one step at a time. First, he needed to free her. Then he could worry about what it all meant.

"She has been here a long while, Alpha," Egros said and examined the chains and the runes on the wall, "these symbols are both Native American and European. I suspect the woman here is descended from both sides. Judging from her dress, she was probably confined here sometime in the late eighteen-century."

"Why isn't she waking up?"

"I am not sure, sir," he said, "but I have an idea."

The twinkle in the Guardian's eye left Kingston with little doubt where his thoughts were headed. The others all seemed too stunned to speak, and he couldn't blame them. For years they'd thought he was mated to the one the universe had deemed his one and only.

He'd allowed them to believe that. Had lied to them all. Kingston could hardly accept it. He knew deep down he was not worthy of his own mate.

"We are not qualified to decide who is worthy, Alpha," Egros said quietly, "the universe knows better than we do."

"Boss, is she really your mate? What about Neela?" Furio asked and he could hear the confusion in the Stallion Shifter's voice.

It was no more or less than what he was feeling himself. All he could do was nod in answer.

"Shh," Storm hissed at the Stallion.

"You have to claim her then," Fergie said and from the muffled sounds coming after that statement, Kingston could only assume Storm had covered his mate's mouth with his hand.

"Ouch!" the Wolf growled and hopped on one foot after his mate stomped on his booted appendage with her stilettos.

Kingston wished he had on shoes, but a quick look told him his own mate was barefoot. Perfect. Maybe that would save him from her wrath after he did what he was about to.

Shit. His body trembled and his Dragon snarled. Worthy or not. Time was up. She needed him and there was nothing he would not do for her.

"Kingston," Byram interrupted, but he was not in the mood for the Vampire.

"Everyone leave," he growled, allowing only a fraction of his Alpha's powers to seep into his voice.

When no one moved, he tried again, this time using triple the amount of command as he bellowed, "OUT! NOW"

Chapter Four

Holley could feel her mate pressing in on her in the dank and cold dungeon that had been the prison of her body for nigh on three centuries.

Finally. After decades of visiting him in dreams, he was here, and he was going to free her. She felt the Keep struggling to hold her firmly in place, but this was it. She was certain. He was hers and she was his. Holley was finally going to be free.

Let me go now. He is my mate. She pleaded with the *manetuwak*, but the spirits of the Keep were not as easy to sway as they had been when they agreed to watch over her.

The Dragon Shifter was mighty though, and she felt his power and the sheer brute force of his strength as he struggled to break the chains that bound her to the stone slab. She pushed the thought at him to use his fire and was surprised when he did.

Even as the others yelled in fright, she loved the image of him maintaining his human form while he called his Dragon's fire forth. Very few managed that sort of control and balance. Kingston Baldric was the only Dragon Shifter she had ever seen, but since the first she had recognized what she was to him.

His Dragon brushed across her mind, the splendid beast growling softly to get near her. Kingston aimed his flames at the metal and after they'd been heated, could then tear them apart. The heat to her had been a mere tickle, but she got the distinct impression that others there would have burnt to a crisp had he spat flames in their direction.

But not him. Kingston Baldric was a seasoned warrior. A noble Guardian, loyal and devoted to his cause. She knew they were fated, just as she knew he would fight it. Her ancestors had told her that when she'd last spoken to them through the veil.

Beware the white-scaled beast, for he has the power to destroy what men and centuries could not.

Those had been her Granny Rose's parting words at their last meeting. Holley never thought much about them, but even as her brain registered that she was almost free, her body seemed downright paralyzed with fright.

"I am sorry about this," the voice of her fated mate spoke as though whispers sifting through the sands of time itself.

She could make out the words, but it was unclear what he meant. Well, it was unclear, until she felt raw pain exploding from her shoulder and travelling through her body at an alarming rate.

She felt fire, his fire, in her very veins. It continued to burn and sizzle until her whole being was aflame. Then there was the flame itself. The spicy, smoky flame of her mate's *Dragon fire* pulsing new life into her body.

She felt her own magic, from both her Lenape and her English roots, rise up to meet his. It was beyond anything she could have ever imagined. A lightning storm of fire and sparkles, flames, and starlight like universes blinking in and out of existence in that single moment suspended in time. It was nothing she could have ever imagined.

Then her back arched and she seized. Her entire body was a mass of pins and needles. Cramps and burning pain filled her. Holley tensed, her back was all the way up, off the stone slab as that lightning strike of flame tore through her.

Her eyes opened wide, but she was still lost in that fierce storm. Unaware of the arms that lifted and held her, the chest that cradled her, and the hands that smoothed across her face.

"It will pass. I got you," a deep, rumbly voice spoke into her ear and Holley relaxed, sinking exhausted into his solid embrace.

It was him. Her own mate. She was safe. She could finally rest, but not before she looked upon him. Willing her heavy lids to open, Holley gasped at the golden-hued stare of the most breathtaking man she had ever seen. Of course, she had seen his face before. Had watched the handsome Shifter for years through the hollows of the Keep, and yet nothing could have prepared her for the impact of his unwavering stare in the flesh.

Her body quivered helplessly as she warmed and swelled in places she could barely comprehend. So this was desire, she thought as her mind raced with a million images of the two of them touching and embracing. Consummating their bond as was their right, their need.

The scandalous image of his naked body flitted through her mind and she felt hot all over. It felt so good, so delicious to be warm again. After centuries in the cold and the dark. Her mind immediately went back to the swell of his manhood she felt pressed against her side.

Holley was a Witch, not a saint. Kingston's lips were a hard line across his chiseled face, and how she wanted to soothe them. To make him smile and laugh.

She had tried to honor the privacy of the Keep's inhabitants, especially during intimate times. But ever since she'd known Kingston Baldric was her mate, she'd tried reaching out to him.

So, yes, she'd spied him in the shower and out. Seen every inch of his glorious naked form. He was a work of art. Sculpted and refined by the finest masters and architects of them all, the Fates, and they had done so just for her.

His nostrils flared as his gaze bore into hers and, though she had no strength to speak of, Holley lifted up in his arms and pressed her mouth to the rigid slash that was his. He was still at first, but the second he understood she was kissing him, her Dragon wrapped the steel band of his arms about her waist and returned said kiss tenfold.

"Mate," he growled and pressed his forehead to hers, but Holley could only sigh before she slipped into the first peaceful sleep, she'd had in three centuries.

Chapter Five

"You need to explain, *cump*," Furio demanded.

"Are you fucking nuts? *Cump*?" Storm mocked his friend and shoved him aside, "He's the leader! Our fucking Alpha, man, and he don't need to explain shit."

"Well, I'd like an explanation," Elena's pink eyes flashed at him, but Kingston was only half listening.

The woman had kissed the common sense out of him then proceeded to pass out. He'd rushed to his suite of rooms and called Egros and Byram to aid his mate. Both had confirmed it was merely sleep.

She was okay. Whoever she was.

Mine, hissed his beast and he closed his eyes against his Dragon's anger.

Possessive fuck that he was, Kingston nodded his head, sating his beast's claim and turned to face his Guardians. What would he tell them? What could he?

Fuck. It was an impossible situation, but they deserved the truth from him.

"I should start at the beginning," he said.

"Good place as any," Fergie smiled, and he snorted at her unique brand of humor.

"Yes, it is," he leaned back in his chair and glanced once at the open door to his sleeping quarters where his mate was curled in the soft six-hundred-thread-count Egyptian cotton sheets.

"When I was younger, my brother and I-"

"You have a brother?" questioned Furio.

"Had," he corrected the young Shifter and his voice filled with sadness, "Edgar was killed many decades ago. A century almost. Anyway, it was before I said my vow to become a Guardian of Chaos. Before I came here to lead you, I was Kingston Baldric of the Skye Clan. I had a brother, Edgar. He and I were more than family, we were best friends, and oftentimes, we were our own fiercest competitors."

"Sounds fun," said Fergie.

"It was," he agreed.

Maybe this wouldn't be so bad, he thought and so he continued, "We shared everything. Games, toys, secrets, hunts, conquests."

"You mean women," said Elena.

"Sometimes," he shrugged, "Our parents passed into the void together as centuries old Dragons sometimes do. We were the last of our kind, the last two Diamond Dragons in the world. Then there was Neela. She was part of our Clan, a rare and dazzling Sapphire Dragon. We competed for her affections-"

"And you won, right boss?" smiled Storm, but Fergie frowned, shaking her head. Women's intuition was real, he mused as she elbowed her mate.

"No, actually, Edgar won her hand," he huffed out a breath and rubbed the back of his neck, "Back then the Skye Clan had opted to stay apart from the troubles of the world, both supernatural and normal. We had no allegiance to either the Guardians or the Loyalists side in the fight against magic, but as everyone knows Dragons are one of the most pure magical beings around, and we are scarce at that."

"How sad," Jessenia murmured, and Furio put his hand on her shoulder in comfort.

"My kind has been hunted and killed for our magic, our fire, our hoards, for thousands of years. It was not long before the Loyalists brought the fight to us. The very day Edgar and Neela made their vows at sunset on the shores of the Atlantic with me as their sole witness, we were attacked."

"Were you prepared?"

"How could we be? We were young and naïve," Kingston's eyes looked at the wall, but in his mind he was taken back to that fateful day on the beach.

Neela was resplendent in her blue sundress with her blonde hair bouncing around her shoulders. She'd cut it shorter than usual and it suited her, Kingston thought as he walked his brother's bride down the makeshift aisle they'd lined with shells and rocks along the sandy beach to where Edgar stood waiting for them.

Barefoot in linen pants and a button-down shirt, his brother's near white hair gleamed brightly in the orange and yellow rays of the setting sun. Kingston was often taken aback at how different they looked, and yet both were Diamond Dragons as their father before them.

His own hair was a deeper, darker shade of blond, almost brown really. Instead of Edgar's blue eyes, his were gold. Both men were tall and fit, as were most Shifters, and even Neela had the body of an Olympian swimmer. She-Dragons were rare and cherished creatures, and envy stabbed at him at his brother's good fortune.

A truth which shamed him, so he buried the feeling deep. He knew in his heart that the Fates were tasked with pairing souls, and as much as he cared for Neela, had even once lusted after her body, she was not his. His fated mate was somewhere out there. He had only to find her. But this day was not his, it was theirs.

It was a simple truth. One he took in stride as his brother's blue eyes glowed with his beast as he took his bride's hand in his. Together, the two young Dragons spoke their sacred vows of love and devotion to one another. Kingston knew the mating marks had been exchanged the previous night, but this ceremony was tradition and he stood and witnessed their promise.

The couple gazed at each other with such perfect love and understanding that his Dragon's heart longed for the day when he would make such promises to his own fated mate. How he would treasure her!

Yes, his beast agreed, but his daydreams shattered into a million pieces when they were suddenly attacked. Ambushed by a dozen or so supernaturals wielding magic and weapons. The three Dragons were caught off guard and unprepared to defend themselves, but still Kingston turned to fight, to give his brother and Neela a chance to escape.

Edgar shifted and clutched his mate in his claws, but he was too slow. While Kingston fought off various attacks, a Warlock hurled a magicked spear at Edgar. He had been aiming for Neela. She was most vulnerable, unable to shift as quickly as her male counterpart, and Edgar had thought to fly her to safety. Instead, he'd put her in greater danger. At the last minute, his brother turned his enormous, scaled body and bared his side where he was most vulnerable, taking the hit himself.

After Kingston had finished off his enemies in a berserker-like rage, he went to his brother. Edgar's head lay in Neela's lap and she cried and held him as his life leaked away. He was dying and there was nothing either of them could do to save him.

"Promise me you will keep her safe, King," Edgar begged, "you will take her as your own and guard her with your life. Promise me," Edgar's grip on Kingston's hand was damned near painful, but not as much as watching him die.

It was the way for most Shifters. And for fated mate's, it was worse. Edgar knew what he was asking.

He had to know, but he was counting on Kingston to help him save her.

Neela wept with raw pain as his fire went out, and as she lay gasping, he made up his mind.

"You gave him your word?" Furio asked, jolting him from the past.

Kingston looked up and nodded. Jaw clenched tightly, he looked down at the tight fists he'd unconsciously made on his lap. His claws bit into the soft parts of his palms.

Funny, he didn't even realize he was doing that. Kingston relaxed his fists and watched the droplets of blood well up even as his own healing abilities closed the wounds.

"Oh, Kingston," Fergie said and laid her head on Storm's shoulder, "I am so sorry."

"But you loved Neela?" Elena asked.

"Yes, I loved her, but I was not in love with her. I gave her my bite to heal her, placed her under my protection. I tried. I promised my brother I would save her, and I tried. Afterwards, I joined the Guardians of Chaos to help keep her safe."

"But why? Why did they want her?" Elena asked.

"Because a she-Dragon is rare. They can use her blood and organs in all manner of dark magic,"

Jessenia whispered the answer and Kingston closed his eyes at the thought.

"That's why she was cut up like that," Furio trembled and Kingston could feel his horror.

"Yes," he cleared his throat.

It had taken hours to tell the tale completely, and the sun was creeping up over the forest. Fuck. He had kept these things buried for so long. It was like having a raw wound. One he wished to never feel again. But even as he metaphorically bled, he felt himself healing. This was meant to be. Kingston understood a little better now.

He'd wanted to shield this truth from his Guardians, but it was time to let the whole truth out. They deserved that much.

"Part of what we have uncovered, ever since Fergie was abducted, is that Offner has had his minions out gathering all manner of information on the history of magic in this area. He wants to expand his dark arts, and he's hunting for ley lines. Magical vortexes to further his own stores for whatever hostile takeover he has planned. Dragon blood would only further his cause."

"But she knew this," said Furio, "she knew the risk, so why would Neela go out alone? I mean, one of us was always with her when she went shopping. It makes no sense!"

"She wasn't shopping," Kingston growled and expelled an angry breath.

It was embarrassing, a betrayal of confidence, and his own fucking fault. The hush of silence was deafening and he hated to break faith with her memory, but they all needed to heal. The truth was the only way to do that.

"I failed in my promise to my brother," he announced, "Neela was not shopping, she was in the process of getting artificially inseminated. After a hundred years of being platonically mated to me, she desired offspring. I'd dedicated myself to protecting her, and to serving the Guardians, but I was never able to give her that part of myself. I am not sure she wanted it, per se, as she loved my brother. Still, it is my fault she is gone-"

"What the fuck? No. No fucking way. This is bullshit," Furio pushed off his chair and stormed out of the room.

"I'll go talk to him," Jessenia stood up to follow the Stallion Shifter, her expression somber.

Kingston sighed heavily and looked around the room. Elena's arms were crossed and tears fell from her eyes. She'd known Neela the longest, but not as well as she'd thought.

With his Alpha powers, he sifted through the emotions of his Guardians. He wanted to know how they received this information. Dragons were private creatures. News about his supposed mating to Neela was hard for him to share, and probably just as difficult for them to hear.

"So, Neela wasn't your mate," Fergie said matter-of-factly, "but *she* is?"

Kingston turned to see *her* standing in the doorway. His breath caught in his chest as he took her in. Familiar long, dark hair floated around her like a cape, and he realized she was standing underneath a vent. She licked her lips, gazing at him with haunted, moss-colored eyes.

"Yes," he answered Fergie's question, but his gaze never wavered from his mate.

She wore an old-fashioned, roughhewn dress that had him frowning at its obvious coarseness against her delicate skin. He wanted to tear the offensive material away from her body and shower her with silks and lace.

Images of her tawny skin naked and bare for his eyes only had his beast hissing and his cock hardening inside his sweatpants. Fuck. He needed to practice better control. Stopping his growling was difficult, even as awareness and recognition passed between them in that long, deliberate stare.

Mine, growled his Dragon.

Kingston waited for her to speak. He swore he saw a hint of a smile playing on the corner of her wide mouth, causing a dimple to pop out puckishly. She turned her gaze to the others in the small sitting room and nodded her head in greeting.

"Well then, it is nice to finally see you all in the flesh," her husky voice broke the silence and it was like lightning struck his every nerve.

Her voice was crisper and deeper than he'd expected, but oh so perfect. His Dragon rumbled in pleasure at hearing the dulcet tones. She walked further into the room on wobbly legs, smiling as she steadied her gait. She looked at everyone, with that open expression and held out her hand.

"I am Holley Mount," she introduced herself, "and I have watched over you with the help of the great *manetuwak*, the spirits of the keep for many, many years."

"Uh, I'm Byram," the Vampire moved first and greeted her politely.

He was quick to shake her hand and let go, which was smart since Kingston had gripped the armrests of his chair tight enough to tear the leather and crush the wood. She turned her head and caught his eye with a perfect black eyebrow arched.

He could not tell if it was annoyance or what, but she continued on. As she had every right to do, he reasoned with his dragon. Hell. He didn't know why she was mad, he was a Shifter. They were possessive assholes at the best of times when it came to their mates.

He cleared his throat, and she turned once to look at him. Then she tilted her head at the damaged chair, and he felt his face heat in embarrassment.

Fuck. He'd have to work on that.

"My name is Egros," the male Witch spoke, and his mate, *Holley*, nodded.

"Yes, you and I must chat about your portal. I think I know a way to make travelling through space and time much more efficient and less draining on your stores of magic," she returned.

"Yes," he nodded enthusiastically, "I would love to hear your thoughts on that."

Like any great diplomat, Holley went to each of the Guardians present. She spoke to them of things she couldn't possibly know, but somehow did. She laughed at something Fergie said and remarked on her vast shoe collection. That earned her a fan for life, he mused.

Then it was Elena's turn. The pink-eyed woman tried to remain stern, but once Holley complimented her on the hours of training the feline Shifter put in to her daily routine, she had her on her side as well. No one took training as seriously as Elena.

"I could show sometime," the woman said and Holley nodded.

"You're Storm," she stopped in front of the Wolf and congratulated him on securing his mate.

Then finally, she was right there. Within touching distance. Kingston held himself very still. One move and he would have her crushed against him.

Fucking hell. He didn't want to scare the woman.

"Hello," she said.

"Hello," he answered.

"So, you said you and the spirits of the Keep watch us?" Fergie asked.

"Yes," Holley said, but remained motionless in front of him.

"Then you do the cooking and cleaning?"

"Not me exactly, but I guide and impress upon the *manetuwak* things that you would prefer."

"Like chicken salad?" growled Storm and Holley laughed.

"Well, it was that, or the manse wanted to suffocate you in your sleep. I thought the food a better punishment, don't you agree?"

"Uh, yeah, sure," he said, and his mate tweaked his nose.

"Okay, you guys have a lot to discuss, so we're gonna go," Fergie announced and began shoving the rest of the lot out of the room.

Thank fuck.

Kingston was barely hanging on to his Dragon. His body vibrated and scales popped out all over his skin. He was hard-pressed not to claim her then and there.

The typically standoffish creature inside of him was snarling like never before. Scratching against his skin with ferocious strength, demanding he fully claim his mate. Now.

Mine.

"I suppose we have things to discuss. Is there anything you want to say to me before we start?"

"Yes," Kingston growled and pulled the woman forward so that she was hovering over him.

He brushed his mouth across hers and it was like the light of a thousand suns burned inside of him. He moaned into her soft mouth as she submitted to his invasion. Tangling his tongue with hers, savoring the flowery blueberry flavor. He kissed her thoroughly before pausing so they could catch their breaths.

His forehead pressed to hers, he said the only word he was capable of, "Mine."

Chapter Six

Holley woke from her unexpected slumber slowly. Had it all been a dream? Was she still chained within the belly of the Keep?

No, she realized as she slowly came back to herself. She was warm for the first time in eons. Everything looked blurry, and she blinked her eyes again until it all became clearer.

This room, she thought, *I know this room.*

Heavy wood furniture without accent or adornment, large windows facing the piney forest, beige walls, plain coverlet on the enormous bed. Yes, she knew this place well. It was *his* room.

Voices from nearby reached her ears, and Holley remained still so she could listen. It was Kingston's voice that sounded loudest to her. That deep timber soothing and alluring. Her chest tightened in sympathy as his words became clear. Poor man, he spoke of his brother and the unusual and tragic circumstances that led to his mating the she-Dragon, Neela.

This group of Guardians had been living within these walls for only a few decades, which to her was relatively short. Decades were nothing to a group of supernaturals with extended lifespans, and certainly not more than a blink to a Witch who'd been captive within the Keep's hollows for centuries.

Still, she'd had an advantage over the Diamond Dragon. Where his hope of finding his own fated mate had been squashed that day with his brother on the beach, she'd recognized what he was to her from the start.

At first, it had broken her heart. She wondered how it was possible that he already had a mate of his own. In fact, Holley had almost gone mad until she saw what really existed between them. Now, she knew the entire story.

Neela and Kingston were bound by a vow neither could break. He'd given his brother his word, gave her his bite to protect her, and in the end neither had been happy. It was all so terribly sad.

Worse still that in seeking some sort of fulfillment away from him, the she-Dragon had been killed. Her life's blood harnessed for dark magic. The guilt he must feel was bound to be overwhelming. Her heart ached for the man.

Holley murmured a small enchantment for the she-Dragon's soul, and another that Kingston might forgive himself. There was no hope for them if he could not move on. Her heart stopped at the pessimistic train of thought.

Technically, she was on borrowed time. Holley was only alive because of magic, but her physical body would wither and age rapidly if their *matebond* was not properly sealed. A bite alone was not capable of that. She was grateful for it, but if Kingston Baldric could not love her, then she would be gone before she ever really lived.

It was easier for her to accept what they were to each other. Truth was, she had fallen in love with him years ago. How could she not?

She knew everything about him. His love for French poetry, war films, and good Scotch. She had the Keep prepare his baths and meals the way he liked them. Knew the telltale signs he gave when he was working out some tough assignment or puzzle. It was all in the way his forehead creased and his smokey scent thickened whenever confronted with something particularly troublesome.

Holley had fallen in love with him in a million different ways. He was their leader, but he was so lonely, so very much *alone*.

She could save him from that fate, but he had to want it. She needed him to open his heart to her in order for them to truly be together.

If there was one thing she knew from watching for all these years, it was that mating without love was worse than pointless. It was cruel. She would not wish that on either of them.

After Holley introduced herself to the people she'd been watching over for years now, she turned to face the man himself.

"I suppose we have things to discuss. Is there anything you want to say to me before we start?"

"Yes," Kingston grunted, then proceeded to kiss the breath out of her.

"Mine," he growled, more beast than man when he finally released her.

Holley swayed on her feet. The man was potent, she would give him that. Her eyebrows rose and she laughed, a short bark of a thing, then covered her mouth quickly with her hands.

"I am sorry, I wasn't expecting that," she said and sat down in the chair across from him.

"No, I apologize really," he tugged on his collar and looked around the room before settling his gaze back on her, " that was my Dragon. He is pressing hard, but I understand you need time-"

"Yes, time," she said and wondered if he knew just how precious little she had.

"Tell me about how you became trapped here," he waved his hand at the room, but she understood his meaning well enough.

"Folks didn't much like Witches in the time I was born," she shrugged, "and half-breed Witches even less."

"Half-breed? Who called you that?" he growled angrily.

"I am sorry, I know it is not, what is it called again? Ah, politically correct, but that is what I was called back then. My father was a Lenape shaman. He fell in love with my mother and together they met in secret. He was killed and the white settlers claimed he had raped my mother. She died while giving birth to me. Sorry, this is a lot of information."

"No, I am sorry," he nodded, "you don't need to apologize for anything. Please, continue."

"I was raised by my Granny Rose. I learned of

my English heritage from her. Magic runs on both sides of my family."

"And how were you trapped here?"

"This place was like a fairyland to me. When I was young, Granny took me hunting for herbs in the woods and we came across it. I knew it was special then, but it wasn't until a demented preacher decided I was unfit to breathe the same air as he, that I set foot inside this place."

"Who was he?"

"Doesn't matter. It was almost three hundred years ago and he can't hurt me now," she offered him comfort with her words, understanding that even if he was reluctant to embrace their relationship, his Dragon would demand justice, "I begged the *mane-tuwak*, the spirits of the Keep to help me and they did."

"I am grateful to them then," he ran a hand through his dark blonde hair.

Holley loved the look of him. His pale skin and light hair, the color of honey, was intoxicating. That and his golden eyes completely through her for a loop.

"I imagine things are going to feel quite confusing for you."

"On the contrary, I have been mindful of the

goings-on within these walls for three hundred years, Kingston. Though I still don't trust tofu, and I am not sure why anyone would 'eat a dick' as Furio is often stating to others, unless he means spotted dick which I know is an English dessert, though I confess it's unappetizing to me, I am very much up to date on current events."

"Uh-"

"I love watching television, and I confess my favorite at the moment are the Jersey Shore reruns everyone binges on in the living room."

"Um-"

"Paulie's hair looks like he got caught in a windstorm with superglue and the women, positively scandalous, but deliciously free. Can I ask what exactly is smushing? I think they mean intercourse, but how exactly is it smushed? And is it related to DTF, or was that GTL?"

"What?"

"Oh, did I go too fast for you?"

"No, not at all, uh, I just didn't know what to expect," he smirked, and she smiled widely back.

The man was simply stunning when he smiled. Holley suddenly felt self-conscious. She tugged on the sleeves of her dress and winced.

"Well, expectations are tricky things. Do you

think? Would it be okay if I took a bath? It has been a long while," she looked down at her scruffy looking feet and bit her lip.

"Of course," he stood up, "I should have suggested it first," he wiped his palms on his trousers.

Was he nervous? She wondered in awe as he took out a small rectangular device and ran his fingers over the screen. It was a cellular phone, she knew, though she had no idea how to use it.

He and the others were always looking at those blasted things. She crept closer to him, inhaling that heavenly smoky scent of his and watched as he used his fingers to send a message.

"I'm asking Fergie and the other women to help get you some things you might need for your, uh, your bath," he growled and she noted the flare of his nostrils.

"Ah, thank you. That is thoughtful," she smiled gently and tried not to frown when he backed away from her.

As a Witch, she had a much more defined sense of smell than *normals* but was nowhere near the level of a Shifter. Unlike other *supernaturals*, Witches were a classification that could encompass a huge variety of abilities. Reading minds was not one of hers, but how she wished it was right then.

"What?" he asked.

"Nothing," she turned and pointed, "It is this way, correct?"

"Yes, let me show you."

Kingston crossed the room and opened the door to his overly enormous bathroom. The claw-foot tub she'd seen so many times loomed ahead, and Holley could hardly believe she was there in the flesh.

Her hands skimmed over the cold porcelain and she closed her eyes, thinking of all the times she'd spied on the Diamond Dragon in the clear depths of the large bathing vessel. She'd imagined herself there with him more times than she would like to admit.

"Have you ever had a bath?"

"Yes," she said indignantly.

"No, I just meant do you know how to turn on the water," he corrected himself.

"Well, we had a wooden tub and filled it from pots. Our baths were usually quite cold, and nowhere near as often as modern times."

"I see," he moved closer, crowding her with his body, and Holley's breath came and went in quick succession.

He was so big, so handsome, she thought as he reached around her back. Her entire being seemed to hum in anticipation, waiting to feel the steady warm pressure of his hands on her. Holley waited, and waited, but he did not touch her. Rather, Kingston turned the handle to the faucet and she turned and gasped. She shrieked happily as warm water cascaded from the spout.

"It's so clear!" she leaned down, very much aware of the near kiss they'd just had and touched the water, "I've seen all these amazing innovations for so many years through the hollows of the Keep, but this is different," she said.

"I'd like to hear more about that," Kingston began.

His voice cutoff when she, without hesitation, pulled the strings that held the simple brown dress together and let the hated thing drop to the floor.

"That will be fine. You can ask me anything," she stepped into the tub, sighing and moaning in pleasure as warmth surrounded her on all sides, oblivious to the glowing eyes of her mate as he stood with his mouth open and stared at her nudity.

"This is divine," she said and turned to look at him, but he was gone.

That was strange.

Chapter Seven

She didn't even notice when he left the room. Caught up in her first-ever modern-day bath, Holley was positively delighted with the wide variety jars and squeezable potion bottles that promised silky hair and smooth skin.

When she was finished, roughly an hour and a half later, Holley had managed to use every single one of them down to the last drop. She thanked the Keep and offered knowledge of her favorites so the *manetuwak* would know which ones to refill.

Steam filled the bathroom. She was loathed to leave the water, but it wrinkled her fingers. Besides, she'd avoided the man long enough. Sighing heavily, she exited the tub and pulled the plug, but before she could do more than wrap an enormous, fluffy towel around her body, the door opened.

"Girl, how long you been in here?" Fergie asked and waved her hands around through the fog.

"What?"

"Come on, we got some stuff," Jessenia smiled at her and Holley recognized the kitchen Witch though she'd been absent earlier when she made her introductions, "We got you some clothes and things."

"Really?"

Holley allowed herself to be pulled forward. She motioned for them to use the sitting room and with a wave of her hand locked the door against anyone else.

"Wow, you can do that?"

"What?"

"Just wave your hand and do cool shit like that," Fergie said excitedly.

"Oh," she laughed indulgently, "I can do some things with magic."

"Why can't you do that?" Fergie asked Jessenia.

"I'm a kitchen Witch, Ferg. how many times do I have to explain that? I make healing balms, and salves, potions, and stuff like that. I don't do that kind of magic," Jessenia said calmly.

"Allow me to explain a bit if I may," Holley said

while she sifted through the piles of clothes the two women had started laying out on the furniture.

"I have both Lenape shaman magic and Lancaster Witch blood running through my veins. I was imprisoned in the Keep before I fully developed my talents, but the spirits herein kept me hidden and safe until such a time I could rejoin life on this plane. My magic developed during my captivity, but I was unable to free myself."

"You needed your mate for that," Jessenia nodded.

"Exactly."

"And that's Kingston?" Fergie asked, seeking confirmation.

"Indeed," Holley bit her lip as she perused the offerings before finally settling on a long soft skirt made up of several ruffled layers in the most lovely print she'd ever seen.

"He's a tough one," Jessenia murmured.

"Pardon?"

"Nothing. Shut up, Jess. Now, don't you love Veronica Beard? These oranges and browns are gonna look gorgeous on you," Fergie held the skirt up to her waist and Holley bit her lip.

"I do not know Veronica Beard, but yes, this is beautiful."

"It was difficult to find petite sizes, but I am kind of an expert being vertically challenged myself," the voluptuous redhead was saying as she handed Holley more things to try on.

She returned to the bathroom, not wanting to disrobe in front of the two females and dressed in the skirt along with a long-sleeved top made out of something called jersey.

Like the state, she thought as she tried and failed to wrestle with the underthings she was supposed to put on beneath the exquisite clothing.

Oh well, she thought, maybe next time. For now, it was enough to be free, washed and clean, and wearing such soft, lovely things against her skin.

"You look so completely hot! Fire breath is gonna bust a vein," Fergie exclaimed.

"Fire breath? Oh, you mean Kingston," Holley felt a deep blush creep across her face.

"Damn straight," the curvaceous redhead pointed to the chair in front of her, "Sit down and we'll help brush your hair."

"Thank you, but I don't want him to bust a vein, do I?"

"Oh, not literally," Jessenia explained.

"It is true I have been watching for centuries, but modern speech is still difficult to pick up."

"I so get that," Fergie said and applied another potion called *leave-in conditioner* to Holley's long locks.

"Hey, you know this hair is awesome, but maybe you should let us trim it?"

"Oh," Holley bit her lip, "like a hair-cut?"

"Yes."

She hated the idea of cutting her hair. But it had been a very long time. Even in that frozen state, it had grown even longer than when she'd last been awake.

"Just a trim?"

"You won't even notice," Jessenia promised.

An hour, and some tears later, Fergie and Jessenia exited the sitting room with a bag full of tags, receipts, and some hair and nail clippings.

"Well?" Kingston's voice reached Holley's ears and she hesitated before stepping out into the hallway behind them.

"Holy shit," Storm said and got an elbow to the gut from his mate.

"Shush up," Fergie growled.

"You wound me, *conpar*," Storm growled playfully.

"Then I better make up for it," she said then kissed him better.

But none of that mattered to her right then, Kingston's golden eyes had found hers. He broke contact, and seemed to trace every inch of her, from her still bare feet to the top of her head with a thoroughness that left her feeling naked.

"You cut your hair," he frowned.

Holley reached up to smooth her hand over the two, long braids she wore on either side of her face. In fact, Fergie and Jessenia had cut about eight-inches off the length of her long locks.

But that hardly made a dent. Her heavy, thick braids hung down to her hips. Only now, the ends were even and unencumbered by something Jessenia referred to as split-ends. A horrible fate that plagued females who spent far too little attention to their own heads of hair.

"Just a little," she waited for his reply.

For some reason, it was very important to her that Kingston approve of her looks. Holley was unlike any of the people there. Her Native American heritage gave her a sharpness to her cheekbones and was responsible for her unique coloring. These things were simple facts and could not be changed or denied.

Instinct told her she would not find racism here among the Guardians, but old habits die hard. She could not be more different from Neela if she'd tried. Even knowing the she-Dragon was not his real mate did not help. After all, he'd been attracted to her and even vied for her attention before his brother staked his claim.

Where Neela was tall, lean, blonde, and beautiful, Holley was short, with small breasts and round hips, tawny skin, a straight nose, and a mouth that was too big for her face. Her eyes were the only appealing thing about her, in her opinion.

The pale green was unusual. Like the lichen or moss that grew in the Pine Barrens. She and her grandmother had often collected such things for salves and other potions.

Granny was like Jessenia in a lot of ways, more kitchen Witch than not. It was her Lenape heritage that afforded her the more unique aspects of her magical talents.

"She looks great," Fergie said with more than a minor annoyance in her voice, "here, try these on," she said and bent down to drop a pair of heels at Holley's feet.

"Oh, um, thank you," she frowned, inspecting the things which to her looked more like torture devices than anything she'd willingly choose to wear.

"Those are from Manolo Blahnik's new line," she

said as if that meant something to Holley who only smiled in response.

With one hand on the wall for support, Holley stepped into the expensive footwear. She gasped at the difference they made in her height. Then stumbled with her first step.

Her eyes went to Kingston's, searching his for anything. Approval, horror, anything at all, but he remained carefully blank as she attempted her second step.

"This isn't so bad," she smiled right before her heel snagged on the thick carpet that covered the hallway.

Holley screamed before covering her face. Hitting the carpeted stone floor was not something she relished experiencing. Lucky for her, she didn't have to. Kingston caught her first.

The rumbling growl in his chest vibrated against her as he took the shoes off her feet and returned them to Storm with a muttered thanks. She clung to his neck, embarrassment still eating at her nerves while he carried her down the hall and out the door.

"Where are you taking me?" she asked, squinting against the bright sunlight.

"To buy you some sensible shoes," he muttered.

"Wait a moment, please," she asked, surprised by

how quickly he stopped in his tracks.

Her heart thundered in her chest and the sound of her blood rushing through her roared in her ears. She was outdoors. For the first time in three centuries. Nerves danced and her belly flipped, but Kingston was holding her. She trusted him implicitly.

"I got you," he whispered as if feeling her anxiety somehow.

She nodded knowingly and Holley tipped her head back to stare at the November sun shining down on her through the tree line. The Keep loomed behind her, she felt its spirits worry and reach for her, but she shook them off. She had her mate now. Everything would be okay. Or so, she hoped.

The big stone structure groaned louder, reaching out for her, but she pushed the tendrils of magic away easily. The castle's magic had grown dependent on her, perhaps even viewed her as its own plaything, but Holley was neither.

She was not a prisoner anymore. No matter how temporary her situation might be, she decided then and there to enjoy every second of it, starting with this.

Sucking in a deep breath, she felt Kingston's eyes on her and nodded her head. He maneuvered her and she slid out of his arms, loving the crush of leaves beneath her feet.

"It is better than I remember," she whispered, opening her arms wide and spinning in a circle.

"What are you doing?"

"Spinning."

"But why?"

"Because the world is beautiful, Kingston, just look at it!" she laughed and continued to move over the leaves in their rainbow of reds, yellows, oranges and purples.

The colors of fall were everywhere. They were there in the bright blue skies, and the warm yellow sun. In the glint of his golden eyes, and the pearly white skin of his cheek. Holley had not felt so alive in centuries.

On and on, she kept spinning, faster and faster, giggling like mad until she almost went down, but he was there once more to save her from harm.

"You are beautiful," he whispered and bent his head.

Kingston's lips were warm and hard. His smoky scent filled her nostrils as he captured her lips in a kiss that warmed her to her soul.

My love, she thought as she kissed him back, *my only love.*

Chapter Eight

ine. Mine. MINE!

Kingston's Dragon was half a second away from busting down the door to his own bedroom. What were those two females doing to his mate?

He heard the squeals and the laughs, and though muffled, he was sure there was some crying thrown in as well. If not for Storm's bemused expression as they waited in the hall, he would've knocked the fucking door down.

Finally, the thing opened and he exhaled. Kingston waited with baited-breath to catch the first glimpse of his sweet mate. The first thing he noted was the now familiar blueberry scent that seemed to tease his senses whenever Holley was near.

Delicious. Mate. Mine, his Dragon hissed.

Nerves danced up and down his spine. Where was she? Jessenia and Fergie had exited first. The two women grinned at each other, then him, stopping for a moment in the doorway.

He wanted to pick them up and move them out of his way. But the idea of touching another female did not sit well with him or his Dragon. He waited, albeit impatiently.

Suddenly, she was there. Kingston's mouth went dry. Bloody hell. Nothing could have prepared him for the sight of his sweet mate after a bath. Her skin glowed warmly, so unlike the pale coldness of when he'd first seen her chained to that hated table.

Her eyes danced over him as she stepped hesitantly into the hall. He swallowed. Hard. The soft, clingy fabric of her top outlined her lovely, firm breasts. She was not wearing a bra. Her nipples pebbled against the material, and suddenly he wanted to claw Storm's eyes out for being there, in the hallway, with them.

Fuck. He had it bad. The possessive urge to cover her and hide her from the prying eyes of others was a genetic throwback to the days of yore when Dragons stole away their maids and hid them amongst their treasure hoards.

Of course, that kind of thing was frowned upon these days. Pity, really. For she was a greater treasure than any he had ever possessed. And yet, something held him back from truly claiming her.

A small, niggling measure of doubt whispered inside his brain. After all, he'd failed Neela. He would fail Holley too. The idea of that warm honeyed glow leaving her skin, that bright sparkle in her eyes dimming forever, made his heart stutter in his chest.

Could he risk it? Risk her life for the sake of his pleasure? What if she was targeted next by Offner or any of the remaining Loyalists?

No, huffed his beast.

He would never let that happen. She would be better off if he never touched her. Decision made, Kingston struggled to keep his beast under control. Resolved to never consummate their mating. To never even lay a hand on her enticingly sweet body.

His jaw clenched, he remained rigid. Unsmiling and unmoving. Well, until Holley attempted to walk in those ridiculous heels that Fergie had given her. He was fond of the redhead, but those things were lethal weapons.

The damn spindly contraptions got caught on something, perhaps the carpet that ran throughout the hallway. As she pitched forward, Kingston threw his resolve out the window. He could not allow her fragile, soft body to hit the hard, unrepentant floor. Not while he still drew breath.

With faster reflexes than ever before, Kingston covered ten feet of space in a nanosecond. He heard the surrounding gasps, registered that something unique was happening, but nothing mattered until she was safely in his arms.

"*Cump*, look down," Storm whispered, pushing his mate behind him.

Kingston growled softly but did as asked. Good thing too, he mused. Orange and red glowing flames swirled around him, surrounding his entire body.

"I think he got blinky," Fergie whispered.

"What?" he asked.

"Like Hudson. But instead of blinking, you kinda burned through space and time. I mean Kingston, you were there one second then the next you were over there and carrying Holley," the redhead said unable or unwilling to hide the amazement in her voice.

Yes, his Dragon chuffed.

He had burned across the hall to catch his precious female. Once in his arms, those same glowing tendrils circled the two of them. For a moment, he wondered if the fire would hurt her, but it did not seem to, though the wall was taking a bit of a beating from the heat.

"It's lovely," she said and leaned her face closer to his, laying her head down on his shoulder.

His chest swelled with ride. She was simply beyond his experience with women. Unafraid of fire, perfect for a Dragon. How could he ever let her go?

Mine.

He felt her magic reach out to his. Touching, swirling, moving in and out of one another. It was intimate. It was incredible. And for a single breath of time, it combined, pulsing in time, before it stopped and faded away.

Holley's impossibly pale green eyes met his for a moment before she wrapped her arms around his neck and crushed her small, firm breasts to his chest. He returned the embrace, holding her tight to him. His precious mate.

She felt so fucking good, wound around him like that. Far too good to let go. No, he would not even consider it again.

Fuck those shoes though, he thought and began to stride purposefully down the long corridor with the exit in mind. He knew the Keep had a way of playing with individuals who had no clear destination.

Kingston always had a goal in mind, and this was simple. Get Holley comfortable, *and safe*, footwear. Done and done.

What he was not prepared for was how beautiful she looked reacting to her first time outdoors in almost three hundred years. The Diamond Dragon inside of him stirred and puffed out a short flame to celebrate her joy.

Fuck yes, she was joyous. Glorious really. Spinning among the leaves, looking for all the world like the brightest, most precious quantity among the jewel-toned world that was New Jersey in Autumn.

Bathed in the warm sunlight and dancing barefoot among the fallen leaves, Holley Mount, the newly freed Witch, captured his tough Dragon's heart without even trying. If he were being honest, she'd had control of the organ since the moment he'd entered the dungeon-like prison where she'd been hidden all this time.

No wonder he'd insisted on coming here, on gaining this assignment. Somehow, deep within, he'd known she was there. His Dragon had recognized the Keep as his home because of her. It all made sense now.

If only he were worthy of her.

Grrr. The beast inside of him hissed at his

defeatist remark. The creature wanted to kick his own ass for all his doubt. He knew it was true, the Dragon would gladly pound out any uncertainty that he was man enough for the job of loving her with his own claws.

Fuck. *Am I strong enough?* He wondered for a brief moment, hating his vulnerability.

Only one way to find out, the Dragon growled.

Chapter Nine

Holley sat stiffly in the strange vehicle, chewing on her lower lip. She had seen cars on television, but she had never been inside of one. The seat was soft and comfortable, and there was some sort of magical inner heating device that warmed her bottom.

She didn't think she would ever get enough of feeling warm, though nothing topped being inside her Dragon's arms. Maybe it was too soon for that, but he had been hers since she saw him all those years ago when he'd entered the doors of the Keep.

So handsome and stern. Then Neela had stepped inside behind him and Holley's heart had damn near been ripped out of her chest. Time had a way of being lost in the belly of the Keep, but she knew it had been many moons before she understood what they were to each other.

Mated, but not. Bound, but apart. Her heart ached for Kingston in those times. He had struggled to maintain balance, to keep the woman, Neela, safe and protected.

Shifters readily accepted *matebonds* as wonderful things, but what they did not perhaps recognize was that the magic that tied two souls was not without a price. Nothing was.

When Kingston had offered Neela his bite to honor his brother's dying wish he had given a piece of his life's force to the woman. That bond that kept her alive and stopped her from following her fated mate unto death had to feed from something. That something was him.

"What you did was an incredible sacrifice, Kingston, for Neela."

"I'm sorry?"

"I know the pain it caused you, the toll it took on you physically and magically, and Neela knows it too. She honors you, Kingston," Holley closed her eyes and allowed that knowledge in.

"How do you know that?" he muttered.

"I know a lot more than you think," she clutched the armrest.

Cars were fast on television, in real life they moved incredibly so. Certainly far too quickly to be safe.

"Are you alright?" Kingston asked from his position behind the wheel of the Mercedes.

"Um, yes?"

It came out as a question, and she supposed it was. Her stomach was in nervous knots. Holley's heart was pounding furiously inside her chest, and truthfully, she did not know if she was alright.

"Want me to slow down?"

"No! Please don't."

The man beside her focused on driving and she allowed him some space. After all, it was probably not easy for him to consider the situation they were in. Though her heart hurt because she wanted him to feel nothing but joy when he looked at her, she understood his melancholy.

Time, he needed time. As for her, there was much to explore and experience. Being back in the world was a gift she had no intention of wasting.

"Almost there," he murmured.

Holley leaned on the leather covered door to stare at the scenery as it sped by as they drove in to the city. She made herself dizzy in the process. So many people, so many buildings. They were crowded and busy, and oh so splendid!

She yelped when the clear glass buzzed and began to slide into the door. Afraid, she broke the thing; she looked at Kingston who smiled and demonstrated on his side.

"This button controls the window. You can lift it up to close it again if it is too cold-"

"Oh no, I love it," she laughed as the cool Autumn breeze flew inside the vehicle, chilling her skin and whipping her braids behind her.

The look on the Diamond Dragon's face as he watched her made Holley's stomach flip. Of course, that was for another reason altogether other than nerves.

She was a maiden still, even after three hundred years, but she understood the heat in his dragon's gaze. That golden glow that spoke of his physical appetites and lust for her. How thrilling!

The Keep allowed her to see many things during her captivity. Though she tried not to spy on private moments, she had not been altogether innocent. Well, a girl had to get her education somewhere.

Mostly, that was from television. Holley arrived at the conclusion that sex was fast, messy, and altogether something she desperately wanted to experience in the present.

The Guardians had eclectic tastes in entertainment. And while she sometimes watched Elena's suspense thrillers, she often found herself watching rom-coms with Fergie. TV was marvelous in her opinion, as were books. But it was hard to open a book when you did not exist in reality.

Now that she did, she had hundreds of volumes on her list. Something she could not wait to indulge in. Kingston enjoyed books, but rarely had time. He never seemed to watch television.

Byram however was an aficionado of something called erotica films that often involved graphicly detailed scenarios that Holley could hardly comprehend. Who knew a human being could contort themselves into such shapes?

Still, something about everything she had witnessed triggered a response deep within her woman's soul. Curiosity mainly, but it was more. Longing, desire, the need to complete the mating bond they'd begun when his bite broke the spell that kept her captive to the Keep.

The spontaneous kiss they'd shared had awakened something inside of her. Something primal and fierce. She knew times were different, but she could not help but tremble at the idea that a woman, that she could want someone in such a carnal way.

And yet she was certain he was the only man she would ever want. The only man whose body she wanted claiming hers in every way that mattered.

Holley had accepted his kiss with enthusiasm, if not skill. But something had him ending the exchange far too soon for her liking. Maybe her inexperience was unattractive to a worldly Dragon? She would have to ask Fergie or Jessenia about that when they returned to the Keep.

Meanwhile, she would enjoy this outing. Kingston's smoky scent teased her senses in the closed confines of the luxury automobile, and she almost missed his question.

Holley was a daydreamer by nature, but now she was trying to distract herself from carnal thoughts whilst in his company. It was proving a most difficult job. He was so, what was the word, ah, *blazing*.

Yes, that was what Fergie had said. Her delightful vocabulary was the cause of much entertainment for Holley. But she agreed with the she-Wolf, her mate had certainly set her heart ablaze.

"Is there anything else you can think of that you need? Besides shoes," he glanced at her bare feet and rolled the car to a stop in front of a store with an enormous sign that read *Victor's Shoes*.

"No, I don't think so," she answered.

"Right," he nodded and walked around to her side of the car, opening the door for her and lifting her out of the seat before she could step on the ground.

"People are staring."

"Let them," he replied in a husky whisper that sent shivers down her spine.

Holley leaned forward but the moment was gone. He turned and carried her into the shop, placing her on a bench while he spoke to the proprietor. She saw in the man's aura that he was a Shifter. Badger was her guess from the scent and the general ornery *tsk* that followed every curt phrase.

"So, you need to be measured? Don't know your own shoe size then?"

"I am sorry, I-"

"You don't have to apologize. Victor, you are being rude," Kingston growled.

"Oh hush, I'm just playin' with the girlie. Come on, let's see what you've got. Size nine! For a petite thing you have a big foot, lady. What?" Victor whistled at Kingston's growl and shook his head, "Fine.

No more commentary. I'll see what I have in back for you."

"Comfortable shoes, Vic, none of that nonsense Storm's mate prefers," Kingston ordered.

"What if I want that nonsense?" she asked, eyebrows raised.

"Do you?"

"No."

Kingston raised one eyebrow, giving himself an air of arrogance that she would have found obnoxious on anyone else. But he was right. Holley did not want high heels. She did want something though. Not nonsense. Him. Only him.

Kingston's nostrils flared and his golden eyes glittered at her in the dimly lit shoe store. For a moment, a wave of dizziness swept over her. She closed her eyes and steadied herself.

She wasn't prone to headaches, but after all, this was her first adventure outdoors in two-hundred and seventy years. Her stomach rumbled, and she covered her lips at the audible sound.

"Are you okay?"

Kingston appeared at her side.

"Yes. I am sorry, where are my manners?"

"Who cares about manners? You're hungry. I

should feed you," concern darkened his gaze, and she gasped.

From what she knew of Shifters, if he accepted her as his mate, his knowledge of her needs and desires would only grow. So far, he'd kissed her once and seemed entirely unaffected, but maybe she was wrong. Maybe he wanted her just as much as she wanted him.

How could she tell? She licked her lips and watched as his eyes followed the movement. Holley was on borrowed time, but she couldn't tell the Diamond Dragon that. Would not force him into making another sacrificial mating. It would be too much like what he'd already gone through.

She could never do that to him. Not after loving him from afar for all these long years. The way he gripped her hand now was definitely promising. She had some time yet. Perhaps it was possible he cared more for her than he was letting on?

"I am a little hungry, I think," she confessed.

His face remained unsmiling as he brought one long, masculine hand up to caress her cheek.

"We should head back. I am sorry, I didn't think-"

"No, I love being outside."

"Holley, it's too much for you. I should have made sure you ate breakfast first-"

"Please. I want to stay out. We can get something to eat, can't we?"

"Yes. That's a possibility."

"Thank you," she whispered huskily, "You have no idea what it was like."

"I can't imagine," he smiled kindly.

"Here you are," the stout shopkeeper came into view with a wheeled cart full of boxes.

Holley laughed in delight as he opened each one, displaying a variety of different shoes and boots all made to fit her feet. Imagine that!

"In my day, common folk were lucky to have slippers made of woven cloth or rough leather with thin soles that wore out quickly," she exclaimed as she lifted shoe after shoe out of boxes made of something called cardboard.

"In your day? What are you, twenty-five?" Victor rolled his eyes and walked away to answer the ringing phone.

"Sorry," she grimaced at Kingston who waved away her concern.

"Don't worry about him. Go on, I like hearing about your day."

"Well, only the rich had heels and soles, and

those were made of wood covered in silk and calfskin with buttons and lace. Not me, of course."

"Why not you?"

"Oh," she frowned, "Well, I was an outcast for my entire life. Granny Rose kept us fed, but only just."

"I am sorry."

"Don't be."

It was true, there was a time she had hated her circumstance of birth, but only briefly.

"I was angry about it once, but I don't feel that way now."

"How come you're not bitter?"

"Because," she shook her head and stood up, walking over to him, "I have a chance at life now. I spent decades just watching, but I am here now, and I am breathing the same air as you, hearing the same sounds, seeing the same things-"

"You can't possibly see what I see," he said, and his eyes glittered as they seemed to devour her from head to toe in the closed confines of the shop.

Holley's chest heaved with the efforts of breathing, and she understood then what it was to be in the eyeline of a predator. Kingston was part beast, and his Dragon was watching her from behind golden eyes that seemed to see far too much.

"I like these," she grabbed a pair of something called Converse and held them high.

"Those are classics," he grinned.

"But how does a shoe converse with its wearer? Perhaps a Witch created these?"

"She wants those?" Victor came wheezing back into the room and looked sideways at her choice.

"You heard the lady. Get her a dozen pairs, one in every color. How about boots for the snow and rain?" Kingston asked.

Holley nodded demurely and accepted his offer of the extra pairs of shoes. It was extravagant, in her opinion, but he insisted.

"Well, you're gonna need socks," Victor waved to the wall where dozens of clothing called socks hung on tiny plastic hooks.

Holley was amazed at the variety. Each one was so different! There were tall socks, and short, something called no-sees, and dozens more.

"They're like stockings," Kingston explained when the little man left to gather her things.

"Yes," she nodded.

The colors and patterns were extraordinary! Holley had seen them on television often enough, but in actual life, they were something else.

"Can I, uh, can I touch them?" she asked and held a hand out tentatively.

"Of course," he sounded angry, but she was so intent on a pair of little white socks with tiny dragons in every color of the rainbow to notice.

"Take as many as you want. Victor! Add these to the total and bill my credit card. I'll carry these boxes to the car."

"Okay," Holley bit her lip and made her selections once he was out of sight.

By the time Kingston came back inside, she was tying the laces to a pair of forest-green Converse into two lovely although misshapen bows. A plastic bag filled with her secret hoard of dragon socks sat next to her, but she carefully avoided bringing any attention to them.

"You ready?" Kingston grunted.

Holley nodded and stood up, moaning loudly at the sinfully comfortable shoes. He growled in his throat and headed for the door, shoving it open with a loud crash.

Holley jumped and followed happily oblivious to his state. Kingston strode purposefully towards the car, leaving her to follow behind him, and she suddenly wondered why he was so angry. It had happened out of nowhere!

He didn't look at her. Wouldn't talk to her. And why? What had she done wrong? In her opinion, not a darn thing. But still, she worried and frowned, chewing on her lower lip as she did whenever she was nervous or contemplating something puzzling. The scenery was not that interesting anymore, not when faced with the conundrum of a Dragon's moods.

Sigh. First hot, then cold, not hot for a different reason. Would she ever understand this man? Could she win his heart? Perhaps honesty would be best. Maybe she should just come right out and admit her feelings.

It was new to her, this uncertainty on how to proceed. Nothing had ever mattered so much to her. Yes, Holley had fought for her life, but this was different. Now, she was fighting for her love.

She played with the little button that controlled the window as she contemplated her situation. Kingston was a man and man followed base instincts. Perhaps she could appeal to those first, then make her case. But how?

She was not exactly schooled in the arts of seduction. And the idea of using feminine wiles to woo the man left her mouth dry and goose pimples running up and down her arms. Up and down, she flicked the button only stopping when he slammed on the brakes and caused her to spill forward slightly in her seat.

"Up or down. Pick one," he growled.

"Fine," she answered with no small amount of cheek, opting for down.

The glass was clear, but she'd been gazing at life from behind a veil for far too long. The air had grown chilly while they were shopping, but she didn't care.

It felt good. Time to save her worry for another day, she decided. Holley smiled and waved to people as they drove past. She didn't understand why they frowned and pointed, but that was alright. She was free. She was happy. And she wanted to share her good spirits with the entire world.

The traffic light ahead of them flashed red and Kingston stomped once more on the brakes. Holley held her hands out to keep from slamming into the dashboard this time.

Heavens, he was upset, but her curiosity was soon overpowered by a sudden undeniable hunger. Not for him. For food. Her stomach growled loudly as the most delicious fragrance she had ever encountered filled the car.

"Oh heavens! What is that smell?"

"What? Holley!"

He yelled her name and tugged on her skirt, but she already had her entire head out the window and was sucking in great, greedy gulps of air to satisfy her curiosity. The aroma was cleverly executed. A delicate balance of several fine ingredients. The result made her mouth water.

Contrary to the Guardians' belief that the Keep's kitchen was operated by one source of magic, Holley knew that was not true. Yes, she had coaxed the castle into punishing Storm by denying him his favorite meals on one or more occasions. And yes, she did encourage the Keep to listen to their wishes and cravings as it was her firm belief happy stomachs led to happy Guardians. But she was not the cook.

Not being able to taste anything would grossly inhibit her ability to produce anything edible. To be honest, cooking was never her forte. She did dabble in the kitchen arts, her talents lie mostly in healing salves and ointments, and some other areas. Like precognition and necromancy.

"Are you talking about *Pizza Palace*?"

She turned and looked at him. He was staring with one eyebrow raised perfectly in inquiry. He was so handsome.

"Pizza?" she turned back to the window, "is that what smells so wonderful?"

That was pizza? She had seen it on TV but had never smelled such deliciousness in life. Unfortunately, food in the eighteenth century was more perfunctory than appetizing.

Oh my. Was that fresh garlic? And yeast dough? Oh yes. With tomatoes? And basil? Sigh.

Holley was practically drooling. Her stomach rumbled once more. She felt her cheeks blush and hid her face when Kingston's lips quirked. She peeked though. Couldn't help but watch as his emotions flitted from shock, to amusement, and finally, indulgence.

"I suppose I can take you to lunch, since I did rush you out the door without breakfast," he put the vehicle into park once more.

"That would be lovely," she answered.

"Yes," his gaze watched her hungrily, and for a moment Holley thought perhaps pizza wasn't the only thing that appealed to the big man.

The possibility made her shiver in awareness and anticipation. But first things first.

"Hi! Sit anywhere you like," a woman dressed in jeans and a t-shirt bearing the Pizza Palace logo waved them to the dining area.

"Is this a date, then?" Holley asked when he guided her to the booth and helped her slide in.

"A date?" he cocked his head and his dusky blonde hair brushed his shoulder, "I suppose it is."

Oh my.

Chapter Ten

Bloody fucking hell. He should have just kicked his ass earlier like his Dragon wanted to. It would have been less painful than what he was experiencing at the moment.

Reaching beneath the table, he adjusted his jeans, but it was no use. He was cramped and stifled in the tiny booth, and his dick was harder than steel, and the woman across from him was the cause. Of course, it wasn't the booth's fault. Not exactly. It was the woman sitting across from him. She was the cause of his current state.

His Dragon growled. He was conflicted. There were too many people there. Too many witnesses to her sweet moans as she sampled bite after bite from the three large pizzas he'd ordered, along with a huge antipasto salad, and a basket of garlic knots.

The feast was spread out between them across the table and Holley seemed to be having the time of her life.

"All this is just for us?"

"Yes."

"Well then, let's eat."

She seemed particularly fond of the veggie lovers' pie, where he was strictly a pepperoni and hot cherry pepper kind of guy. She'd *oohed* and *aahed* her way through almost every dish. Her reactions dazzled him. He'd never seen someone enjoy food so much. And he was a Shifter, for fuck's sake.

Of course, he wasn't even going to mention the pineapple topped monstrosity in front of them. That was the one item that still remained untouched.

"Don't say 'I told you so', honestly, I meant to try it."

"Yeah, I know, but, *I told you so*," he winked and took another well-done slice of pepperoni for himself.

Judging from her reaction to the spur of the moment gesture, he was positive he'd shocked the little Witch. About time. The way he figured, she'd been driving him out of his mind with every excited giggle, soft sigh, and delightful moan that escaped her delectable lips throughout the meal.

"What?" she asked, "Is my face dirty?"

"No. Your face is perfect," he confessed.

It was only the truth. Funny how easy it was to compliment her once he started.

"I had a good time today, taking you shopping, eating pizza with you here."

"Ah, yes, and teaching me to drink through a straw," she blushed and shook her head, but it was the truth.

He'd enjoyed showing her the options and watching as she chose the metal kind rather than the disposable. He wasn't in to killing turtles either, thank you very much.

The simplest things proved to be more adventurous than he'd ever thought through her eyes at her side. Fuck, everything she did turned him on. Her reactions to the modern world were so open and honest.

Refreshing, that was the right word. There was none of that second-guessing or mockery he found in so many others. None of the guilt either. That was all he'd felt at the end with Neela. Terrible, overwhelming guilt.

"It wasn't your fault," Holley whispered.

He nodded his head, a reflex really, but the she-Dragon had been his responsibility for so long. It felt disloyal to think about her like that.

No, his Dragon rose up and pushed the thought into his head. Holley was his one true and fated mate. His whole purpose was now dedicated to her and her alone.

"Have you tried these?" he leaned forward and held a garlic knot dipped in marinara sauce to her lips.

Holley moaned as she took a bite of the soft, savory dough. She sighed as she slowly chewed the delicious morsel and Kingston was a goner. She leaned forward, took another bite, and his chest vibrated with the force of his growl as he watched.

Great. He was jealous of bread. But what could he say? He wanted to be the one to make her moan like that. He wanted to be everything to her.

Silly? Maybe. Conceited? A little. But fuck it. He had never felt this way about anyone. It was primal and all-consuming, but in the best possible way. She was everything wonderful in the world. Watching her enjoy herself with the food he provided pleased his beast. At the same time, it was also the most torturously erotic thing he'd ever witnessed.

What about Neela? What about the past? What about her, he argued with himself. She was gone. He'd done his best to do his duty by his brother and by her. The only way to honor them now would be to live.

Yes, he wished he could change the past for both his brother and Neela. To be torn apart from your mate was unthinkable. Edgar thought he was saving her, but perhaps it would have been better to let her go into the void with him. But at the time, it was an impossible choice.

Kingston knew with unwavering certainty that if anything happened to Holley, he would much rather join her than try to live without his mate. That was not something he'd wish on anyone. He would have traded places with Neela if he could. But the fact was, he could not.

Kingston was alive, here and now, and so was Holley. The sweet Witch's blueberry scent filled his senses. Tempting him like nothing else. He found the fragrance lingered whenever she left a room in the most enticing way.

His gaze roamed her face, that healthy glow in her tawny skin, those pale moss-green eyes, and her inky dark hair were all doing things to him he could hardly describe.

Of course they were, the Dragon chuffed. He was born to love her. Fated mates could choose to ignore the pull, but they rarely did. And why should he?

Claim. Mate. Mine.

"Kingston? Are you okay?"

"What? Oh yeah, I am fine."

"You are growling. *Loudly*," she looked around at the tables and he noticed some people were starting to stare as well, "I think they heard you," she whispered.

"Shit. You finished?" he asked, dropping bills on the table when she nodded.

He stood up and held out a hand to help her. Electric shocks danced from his fingertips down his spine and straight to his cock, which had been hard as stone since he'd laid eyes on the beautiful Witch. But he ignored it for now and gently nudged her in front of him so he could follow her out the door.

Her hips swayed beneath the silky skirts she wore and a smile played at the corner of his mouth as he took in the green sneakers. She was cute as hell, sexy too.

He wanted her. Wanted to lay claim to her sweet flesh, to stamp himself all over her body, and to rip the eyes out of every man who dared stare.

He turned his head and flashed his too sharp grin

at a pair of fuckers with a death wish. They yelped and dropped their sodas before rushing down the street. Shit, he had to calm down. It was too soon for this. She needed time. But he did not know how much he could give her.

"Where to next?" she turned and smiled, and because he hated himself, he opened his mouth.

"I know just the place," Kingston took her hand in his and ignored her curious stare when they passed the parked car and walked over to *Dulce's Gelato Bar*.

"Can I have two please? Double chocolate cherry, and one peanut butter swirl," he placed the order and handed her the first cone watching as her eyes lit up at the sweet confection.

Bloody hell. Kingston's eyes crossed as Holley took the cone from his hands. She moaned loudly at her first taste of the frozen treat, giggling when some dripped over the side and ran down her hand.

"Allow me," he said and took the hand, licking off the dribble of chocolate peanut butter gelato.

It was superb, but not as thrilling as having his lips on her. Her eyes caught his, but she broke the contact. Smiling lightly, she licked her cone and walked with him to a small outdoor bench.

All too soon, there was nothing left of her gelato,

so he offered her the remainder of his own confection. He told himself it was because he was a gentleman, and not some pervert. But, *dear gods*, her little moans and groans were doing insane things to him. His Dragon was scratching wildly against his skin. The beast was losing his grip. The primordial imperative to claim her rode him hard, especially when he noticed one or two sets of prying eyes fastened on his delectable little Witch.

Mine. Grrr!

His Dragon was irrationally angry, and there was only one way to satisfy the creature. Kingston stood abruptly and took the cone away from Holley, tossing it in the trash before rushing her to the car.

"I was not finished yet," she licked her lips, frowning at him with a dollop of chocolate still staining the lower.

The urge to bend and lick said lip clean was too much to resist. Kingston wrapped one arm around her tiny waist and tugged her closer to him. Her soft body was so much shorter than his, but still, she felt like heaven to hold.

Mating fever. This was it. That terrible, wonderful madness was taking over, and Kingston went willingly. For her, he would go anywhere.

"I am sorry to rush you, but I have to get you out

of here before I do something crazy," his lips pressed into a hard thin line as he bent lower.

"Like what?"

Need rushed through him like lightning as he placed one hard, urgent kiss against her shocked mouth. But his Witch was nothing if not earthy and warm. She seemed to understand what was happening and opened for him like a flower under the hot sun.

"Kingston," she rested her forehead against his while they both tried to catch their breaths.

"We have to go. Now."

She nodded her head, and he opened the door, tucking her gently inside. Protective instincts he didn't even know he had started to well up inside of him. He drove back to the Keep quickly. The urgency evident in every turn of the wheel and the steady pressure of his foot on the gas pedal.

Scales rippled across his skin only to fade away as he struggled with his beast for control. The Dragon wanted to stake his claim and the mother-fucker did not want to wait.

"Calm now," she cooed to that part of him and his physical response was immediate, "I am yours, only yours," Holley placed one honeyed hand onto his forearm and he hissed in pleasure.

Even the most platonic touch from her was better than a thousand erotic touches from anyone else. He felt his gums throb as his fangs descended. Smoke puffed from his mouth, but all he could utter was a rumbling growl.

Gravel flew across the back entrance of the Keep as he managed, just barely, to stop the car and turn off the ignition before he was out of the door.

Everything got a little fuzzy after that. Kingston remembered opening the door and picking Holley up, princess-style. Recalled quite vividly, the feel of her curvy, warm, petite body in his arms. The dreamy look in her impossibly pale green eyes, and the way her mouth felt when she crushed it to his, imprinted themselves on his brain.

Grrr.

Yes, he recalled the kiss and the faint taste of gelato still on her tongue, but even that sweet dessert could not diminish her flowery-blueberry scent. His Dragon hissed and scratched at his skin to the point where his scales and claws were permanently out, but he was careful with her. He would never hurt the woman who was fated to be his.

"Mine," he growled as he raced towards his room with his precious bundle in his arms.

How he got inside without breaking the door

down was pure magic. Hers to be exact. The woman was a Witch, least he forget. She moaned in sweet submission as he lay her down on the bed, noting with pleasure how the lamps dimmed, the shades closed, and the doors locked.

Thank fuck for that.

It had been an age since Kingston had wanted someone in this way. Dragons had very long lifespans, but a hundred years or more without sex was still a long time. And this was not just sex. This was something else.

"Mine," he said again nuzzling her neck and pressing her down into the mattress beneath him.

They had on too many clothes, he realized quite suddenly and began to rectify that. Feet first, he decided and sunk to his knees, carefully untying the laces of her new Converse.

Kingston froze once they were off her feet. A smile played at the corner of his mouth.

"What's wrong?" she asked, lifting herself up on her elbows.

The blush that quickly followed told him she knew exactly what he was looking at.

"Your socks," his mouth quirked in a grin he couldn't help but allow to spread across his face, "There are dragons on your socks."

"Oh, um, yes," she blushed a darker shade of red and his heart squeezed inside his massive chest.

She was gorgeous. At some point while he was kissing her, he must've tugged the ties from her hair, because it was in beautiful disarray. Thick and glossy, her inky locks were slightly wavy and mussed from his hands. Her lips were swollen and those crazy sexy eyes of hers were sparkling and bright. He'd never wanted someone so much in his entire life.

He tugged off the adorable socks, kissing her pretty feet before running his hands up the length of her calves. Next came her silky thighs and rounded hips as he rose to kneel on the bed. Again, he stopped, shocked at his newest discovery. Kingston's nostrils flared and eyes widened.

"You aren't wearing underwear?"

"Oh," her embarrassment was evident, but she was brave, his Witch, and continued to explain, "well, I couldn't figure out the thong-thing Fergie gave me. I don't know why anyone would want a bit of string in their crack. Seems pointless really," she bit her lip.

"Oh?" he started to laugh, then frowned as realization hit him, "I took you all over town and you were naked beneath this skirt?"

"Well, I suppose, yes."

He hissed audibly, both turned on and exasperated. The Dragon inside of him demanded he mark her immediately. Then. There. Yesterday for fucking fuck.

His mate went outside without underwear and the knowledge made his beast ready to tear the whole fucking town apart in case anyone happened to catch a whiff of her succulent sweet honey.

Mine.

Speaking of her succulent honey. Kingston inhaled and scented her growing arousal. He was hanging on to his beast by a thread, wrestling for control. He didn't want to frighten her. Sweet little innocent that she was, Holley could not know how to handle a Shifter's, especially a Dragon's libido.

It would be pretty damn shocking the first time around for her. He needed patience, tons of it. The need to bring her pleasure, to make sure she was prepared, welled up inside of him.

"Kingston," Holley grinned, and he was the one who was shocked, "I am not a shrinking violet," she said and sat up running her hands over the scales that were once more visible along the skin of his forearms.

"Holley," his voice was little more than gravel at that point.

"I like that your Dragon wants me," she whispered and tugged on his shirt.

He took the hem and tore it off his body. Fuck, her tentative touches were driving him mad. There was nothing he wouldn't do for her. But he was nervous. She was most certainly a virgin, and Kingston had never had to be careful before. What if he hurt her?

Grrr.

"You are so beautiful, aren't you, mate?" she stroked his arms, shoulders, chest and belly.

The Dragon inside of him stirred, perking up with glee. He liked her words. Preened at the attention and praise. Silly fucker.

"So powerful and handsome. Quite the protector too. You would never hurt me, mate. I know that. I trust you, and I have been waiting for you for so long, my own mate," she nuzzled his nose with hers.

He was breathing like a long-distance runner. Kingston could hardly think. She was weaving spells around him. Wonderful, magical, seductive spells and he wanted to go under with her.

More than anything, he wanted to fall into his sweet, warm, intoxicatingly beautiful Witch.

Needed to claim her as his own. To mark her with his bite.

"You know? That we are fated mates? That I woke you with my mating bite?"

Relief coursed through him when Holley nodded. That in turn became something else when next she brushed her wide mouth across his once, and twice, until the temptation was too much to resist.

He caught her lower lip between his teeth, gently tugging until she stilled. Prey to his giant predator. Then he struck, claiming her mouth wholly and fully, and most importantly, with all the desire and feeling he had for her.

"Can I have you?" he asked, as was the tradition with his kind.

"Yes, oh yes," she returned.

After that, it was easy. Phenomenal, but simple. Clothes were shredded, lips were cherished, and bodies moved together in a symphony as old as time itself. Her hair covered them in a warm, thick blanket as Kingston laid down on top of the mattress.

Her kisses left him growling and breathless. He needed her so badly. Wanted her more than air.

Holley's beauty was indescribable through the lusty haze he was under. She was so warm, so bright. All golds and browns, skin like honey against his own alabaster flesh. She was divine, but earthy too. Her magic hummed all around them, cocooning them in a bubble where only they two existed.

It was the only place he ever wanted to be. Kingston suckled her dusky breasts, taking the firm nipples between his lips and using his tongue to make her moan.

Fuck, she even tasted like blueberries and her flowery scent deepened with her growing passion. His Dragon snarled impatiently. He wanted to savor, but his beast demanded he claim her first.

"Want you, please," she said and slid her dripping sex along the length of his cock.

Fuck, he went cross-eyed. She was so fucking hot. Sexier than he'd ever imagined was possible. Running on instinct, not practice, and wasn't that better than anything?

"Kingston," she moaned, and he nodded.

"Yes, take me inside you, mate," he whispered huskily, guiding her hand to his cock.

"Don't know how," she gasped, holding firm to the base of his cock as she continued to slide her heated sex along its length, "oh gods, Kingston, this feels so good."

"Lift up, baby," he coaxed and placed the head of his cock at her entrance.

Her eyes opened and hands gripped his shoulders as his mushroomed head pressed inside of her tight sheath. Holley whimpered in her need and uncertainty. Her nostrils flared, but he was there for her. He would always be there for her, he vowed

"You were made for me, Holley. Press down when you are ready, so you can control it," he spoke through gritted teeth.

Brows furrowed in concentration, it took all his strength and control not to simply thrust upwards, but that would make him a greedy dick. And he would never hurt her or risk what they had by being impatient.

Fuck, this was going to kill him, but it was such sweet agony. Holley's face was flushed. Perspiration dotted her forehead as she did as he said and pushed down.

Eyes bright, she groaned and pushed past the pain. Fuck, she was so fucking tight. He went cross-eyed, but he stayed focused. He didn't want to hurt her. He could never live with himself if he did.

Holding himself still, he allowed her the time she needed to adjust to his size and girth. Kingston reined in his beast and concentrated on her. Sitting up on the mattress, he held her hips between his massive hands and whispered words of encouragement in her ear.

She was so small, so perfect. Holley grunted and clutched his shoulders. Her fingernails bit into the skin there. Her moss-colored eyes held his, and he growled at the pain he saw in them as she took the final plunge. Pushing past the barrier between them, Holley impaled herself on his cock.

Fuck, it felt so good to be inside her heated sheath. She was so tight, so fucking perfect.

"Agh," she cried out.

Kingston held her in his arms and kissed her slowly, swallowing the small sound. Still, not yet daring to move, Kingston stroked her hips and back, the globes of her ass, kissing her lips, then her neck. He caressed and stroked her breasts, kneading the mounds until she was moaning and relaxed against him.

"That's it, baby, you can take me. Relax your muscles, easy," he moaned, praising her and calming her.

He felt her magic pulse around them as her body adjusted to his invasion. Soon she was kissing him back. His hands swallowed her pert breasts. He squeezed and plucked her nipples, loving her groans.

His tongue scoped every inch of her mouth. Her response was immediate and sublime.

"So good, baby," he growled and felt a flush of warmth as she rocked her hips. Slowly, he began to move and she with him. Coating his cock with her juices as she accepted him fully and completely.

Thank the gods.

Chapter Eleven

olley could hardly catch her breath. This was real. It was happening. After decades of watching her heart's desire, she was with him now. Her fated mate was in her arms, and it was the most profound moment of her existence.

His smoky scent invaded her nostrils. The taste of his lips as they moved over hers was sublime. Physical love was something she was very curious about, and now she knew.

Even with her imagination and decades of reading books over shoulders and watching television could not have prepared her for the sensual onslaught that was being claimed by her Dragon.

Her heart was liable to beat her to death in the process, but it was worth it. So worth it.

She moaned as Kingston's enormous girth stretched and filled her most secret places. She'd learned a lot about sex during her captivity in the hollows of the Keep. But TV and books had nothing on this.

Holy hell! She'd never spied on the Guardians during their naughty times, but even if she had. Nothing could have readied her for the intensity of his enormous cock stretching and filling her, stroking inside her depths with such precision as to send lightning strikes of pleasure coursing through her veins.

Kingston's throaty growls were doing things to her she could hardly comprehend. He was so beautiful, so magnificent. She wanted to shower him with affection, show him what he meant to her.

Love filled her as she stared in awe at his big, warm body, pale against the bronzed flesh that was her birthright. A fact she could not change or hide. And she didn't want to. People of her time period had sneered at her in hatred, but not him.

The golden eyes of her Dragon lover seemed to covet every inch of her honeyed flesh. Holley was more than willing to give it over to his expert handling. His kisses seared her very soul. He was temptation personified. More than that, he was love. Her love. Always.

"Want you to claim me, mate," she said, egging on his beast, wanting more of him as her magic pulsed in time with her jerky movements.

"Mine," he hissed and flipped them over.

Beneath him now, Holley arched into his flexes. he was able to fill her much more deeply now, and he moaned at the sensual invasion that was Kingston taking over her every cell.

Oh my, he was heaven and hell, angel and devil, all rolled into one, she thought as he brought her heated body to heights she'd never imagined.

"Kingston," she cried alarmed at the sensations rolling through her.

Her stomach tightened, heart raced, and a tingling, burning need began to throb from her sex throughout her entire being.

"I got you, mate, I will always have you," he groaned as he reached between them, flicking her sensitive flesh with his thumb. And then, she saw stars.

A sharp, distinct pain exploded in her shoulder, before turning into the most exquisite pleasure. He did it. He bit her. Making it even sweeter as he lapped at her flesh, sealing the mark from his bite, and completing their *matebond.*

"Mine," he snarled and fastened his mouth to hers as he pumped his hips and spurred on another orgasm that left her gasping for air.

Kingston's body went rigid, and he roared aloud, emptying his seed into her womb. Holley held him through it all. Every shiver and tremble, rippled and convulsion of their joining brought more pleasure and fulfillment than she could've ever imagine. She kissed his face, his shoulders, his chest, anywhere she could reach, even as she struggled for breath. His scales were out once more, and she loved knowing the Dragon was there with them.

"I'm yours, mate," she soothed him with her words, her kisses, and long strokes of her hands on his back, shoulders, and finally, his brow.

"Mine," he said and struggled to steady his breathing.

"Yes," she smiled sleepily against him.

She wanted to stay awake, to talk about what this meant, to tell him what she felt, but exhaustion seeped into her bones and she fell asleep cradled in his arms. Cocooned in his arms, safe and warm for the first time in a very long while.

. . .

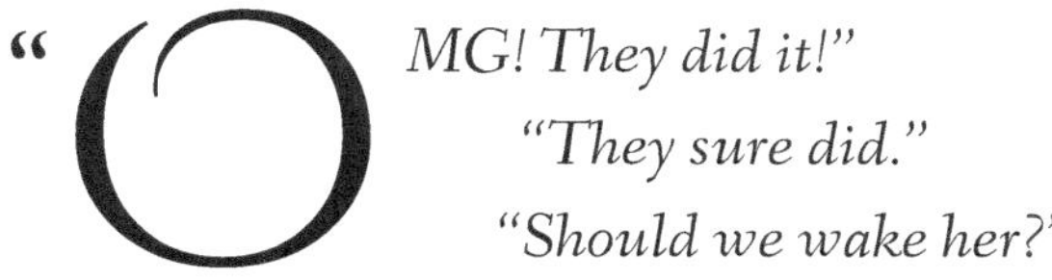

"*MG! They did it!*"

"*They sure did.*"

"*Should we wake her?*"

"*I think we have.*"

Holley blinked slowly against the voices that were disturbing the first good sleep she'd had in a while. She stretched her deliciously sore body and ignored the squeaky yelp that came from her uninvited guests. Fergie and Jessenia were in Kingston's room, and he was markedly absent.

Hmm. So not how she wanted to awaken the morning after being claimed by the magnificent Diamond Dragon, but it was what it was.

Holley turned and blinked at the two women who were facing the wall and not her. Well, at least they were giving her some modicum of privacy. Thank goodness.

"Morning ladies, to what do I owe the pleasure?"

"Holley! Well, I see you were certainly busy last night," Fergie *oomphed* as Jessenia pinched her arm, "What? She was busy."

"Shh. Um, Holley? I was wondering if maybe you wanted to have some tea or something and we can chat?" the kitchen Witch added and glared at her friend.

"Ladies," Holley grinned at their backs and stood up, taking the sheet with her, "How about I take a bath and join you in a few minutes?"

"Perfect!"

"Yes!"

Washed and dressed, Holley walked down the carpeted halls of the Keep by herself to the kitchen. She knew full well to keep her destination in mind. The *manetuwak* or spirits of the Keep were devious tricksters at the best of times, and downright dangerous at the worst. How often had she watched from within as they defeated those who'd dared tried to gain entry without the proper means?

Sigh. Even now, Holley felt the Keep beckoning her back inside, to the safe haven of its hollows that had kept her hidden and secret for nigh on three centuries.

It was difficult, but she was able to resist the pull. She had a mate now. Her connection to Kingston was new, but when she closed her eyes, she could see the ethereal bond that linked their souls, and she knew she was home.

"Thank you, *manetuwak*, you kept me safe, but it is here I belong," she whispered to the Keep as she found the two women sitting at the kitchen counter.

"Please, Keep, I just want to make brownies!"

Jessenia groaned and banged her head on the granite counter.

"What is happening here?"

"Ugh, well, ever since you and Fire-breath were gettin' it on, this is what happened," Fergie said and opened the refrigerator doors.

"What?"

"What do you mean, what? It's empty, Holley! They all are, and I'm starving!"

Holley stared as the bouncy redhead moved to open cabinets and the second fridge, all of which were completely bare.

Darn it. The Keep was angry at her. That much was obvious. But still, it did not explain why she'd woken up alone.

"Um, where is Kingston?"

"How the heck should I know?" Jessenia grunted as she fought to open the oven.

Her bun wobbled on top of her head as she finally got the thing open. But when she went to collect her pan, it was empty.

"What the hell? My brownie mix is gone! Those ingredients were organic, and that was the last of the imported vanilla," she growled and kicked the oven only to yelp in pain.

"Okay, sit down, let me have a look. You know,"

Holley said as she helped the woman to the stool, "this place has a mind of its own and it seems I've made it angry. Still, you should know better than to kick a stainless-steel oven, for goodness' sake."

"I'm sorry. I'm just hungry," mumbled Jessenia.

"Her toe looks fine. Food?" Fergie looked on as Holley inspected Jessenia's foot.

Healing was one of her talents, but they were not needed, she decided and released the appendage. She stood up at once, determining the woman was fine except for a sore ego.

"Let me see what I can do about some breakfast first," Holley announced and was met with a round of applause.

"Is it safe?"

"Of course. That is, I think so," she closed her eyes and channeled those spirits that haunted the halls.

The *manetuwak* were not ghosts, not really, they were *other*. Supernatural creatures, kind of like fairies or very minor gods who used magic to exist on their plane. The Keep attracted them because of where it was located.

Unbeknown to most, the manse was a hotspot of magic. She knew she had to confide in Kingston, had planned to that morning, but he'd already gone by the time the females woke her up.

Typically, the spirits of the Keep offered comfort to those hardworking Guardians of Chaos without whom the particular vein of magic located beneath it would have undoubtedly been plundered ages ago.

You owe it to the Guardians and their mates to keep them fed and cared for, she argued.

But the Keep was being a bit thickheaded. The spirits pushed against her powers. It was as if the manse wanted her back under the spell that had kept her hidden away for so long. She frowned harder trying to convey the importance of her place with her mate.

Please manetuwak, I have a mate now. His job is to protect and shield me. It is not your place any longer. You know I am grateful, but you must resume your duties.

Holley tried for patience, but still the Keep refused to yield. It was taking a toll on her, fighting the thing that had cared and protected her for so long. Her magic was unique, true, but she was out of practice in the real world.

Frowning, she rolled up the sleeves to the soft, pale pink cashmere sweater she wore. The material had felt exquisite against her skin. Especially after such furious lovemaking with her Dragon. She'd relished the smooth, lightweight top the second she slid it over her slightly sore body.

Paired with a long, flowing skirt covered in various hued blossoms, Holley's attention was held captive by the garment for a moment or two. She couldn't help but simply wonder what it would be like to walk amongst such flowers. Finally, she finished the ensemble with a pair of pink dragon socks and white Converse.

Modern day life had its benefits, but clothing aside, she was surprised at what she found in the kitchen. Her new friends were being downright ignored by the very Keep that was to aid and protect them. That would simply not do. She knew that spirits and magic itself could be obstinate, but this was ridiculous.

"You know better, *manetuwak*," she continued aloud, "A promise was made long before I became involved, and that oath holds even now," she closed her eyes in concentration.

"What is she doing?"

"Shhh."

"She is trying to get the Keep to give us back our food."

Holley ignored the whispered voices and

continued to channel the Keep. Pushing words and feelings of praise and thanks to the spirits, she tried to gently remind them of their pledge, asking them to honor that which was set in the very stones of the manse itself.

Unaware of the new arrivals, she could not see the expressions on their faces as her magic pulsed around her in a golden bright aura that was as warm to the touch as it was beautiful. Among them was one particularly curious Diamond Dragon who'd just entered the room to stand with the other Guardians.

Holley felt her hair whip around her shoulders as power pulsed all around her sizzling and crackling like sparks on a fire or some kind of brilliant electrical surge. But she was not cowered by the display, and she had no intentions of giving in to the implied threat. The Keep was throwing a tantrum and she would just have to be stern.

Digging deep within herself, Holley found the thread that tied her to this place. That cord was her connection to the *manetuwak,* the spirits therein. It was what enabled her to live even after being holed up inside the bowels of the manse itself by Preacher Milton and his mad followers.

The memories threatened to shake her nerve, but she pushed them away. He was long since dead and gone. There was nothing left to fear of the man. Grabbing her balls, as Fergie said, she focused with all her might on that single thread.

It was so cold and dark there in that strange realm. The place where magic existed in the physical sense was on a separate plane from the reality she was in now. Holley much preferred the latter, but this place was familiar to her. It was where she'd wandered, much like a ghost, for so many long years.

Watching from afar, waiting for the day she would be free to rejoin the world. The Keep had been both her shelter and her prison. Holley was grateful to the *manetuwak*, but she never wanted to return to the frigid, gloomy place ever again.

Shivers ran through her body the longer she stayed there in that shadow plane. But Holley could not leave just yet. She had to persuade the spirits to honor their path. They had a job to do. They must honor their bargain with the Guardians of Chaos.

Those first warriors who'd commissioned the stone walls and had them built, inlaid with magical properties, had done so long before the Puritans arrived to destroy things one way or another. The *supernaturals* had had an agreement with the native people of the land.

One that would ensure magic remain free and

true. The Lenape understood the necessity and sanctioned construction without quarrel. Yes, Holley had learned much about the history of the Keep.

What she did not understand until right then was that it had hidden itself from Preacher Milton once her own bargain was struck. That was why it wanted her back. To keep her safe. Without her there inside, the spell was broken, and the Keep could once more be found.

The *manetuwak* had vowed to protect her. Yes, its doors would always be open to the ones who'd built it and would use it to keep magic from harm. But somehow, she had become the focus of the spirits within the Keep. Now that her spell was broken, she was at risk.

Holley's mind clouded, and she swayed as image after image of how the Keep had protected her and allowed her to live and retain her youth and her physical body, by suspending it for centuries.

She would grow old now, die someday without them. The idea was scary to say the least. She did not want to die. Not yet. Staying did have its benefits. Yes, they seemed to like that, but something nagged at her mind as the small glowing lights circled her and began to tug on her wrists and hair, pulling her clothing, leading her down the chilled dark path.

"Holley?"

She heard a voice through the mist. The lights swirled faster and faster, picking at her clothes and skin. Wait, a second. No. She did not want to go back to that plane. Not there. Not inside the cold, dark place where she was all alone.

She turned her head in the dimly lit ether and something caught her attention. A thicker, brighter, glowing cord that was pulsating with warmth and heat. It was so bright, so beguiling, she moved away from the mist and the now frantic lights.

Kneeling on the moss-covered ground, she lifted the cord and cried out as the most beautiful feeling she'd ever felt encompassed her. It was like being given life. She was amazed as the sound of her name grew louder.

Holley gasped as she was lifted. She felt the place where Kingston had given her his mating mark burn her skin. That sizzle began to warm her icy flesh, and she moaned. When had she grown so cold? In there, with the lights. She wanted to throw her head back and howl in fury. They'd almost tricked her!

"Holley!" Kingston's voice echoed in her mind as she blinked slowly and looked up into his worried gold eyes.

His Dragon was peeking out at her too, and the beast was not happy. That wouldn't do, she thought, and reached up to stroke his handsome, chiseled face with her cold fingers.

"Calm, my love," she whispered and found her throat was dry.

"Thank the gods," he growled and pulled her into his arms holding her tight to his body.

"What happened?"

"I don't know. We got called away to check out a warehouse for signs of the Loyalists and when I came back you were on the floor, ice cold, and Jessenia and Fergie were trying to wake you up," he said and ran his hands across her face and body, checking for injury but rousing other needs as he went.

"Kingston," she moaned his name and his touch slowed down as he reached her legs.

"You feel so good, so warm," she shivered.

"I'm a Dragon," he growled by way of explanation and she lifted her face for his kiss.

"Ow," she winced as the skin on her shoulder stretched.

She covered her newly opened mating mark with her hand, stunned to see fresh blood there.

"I am sorry, love, I bit you to bring you back," he blushed deeply, and she smiled at him.

"It's alright. I was trying to convince the Keep to take care of you all. It seems the spirits thought perhaps I was not being cared for properly," she tried to explain.

"Well, they can't have you. You," he dropped a kiss on her mouth, "are," and another, "mine," and one more.

Chapter Twelve

Horror. Fury. Agonizing pain.

Those words were hardly adequate to describe the abject fear and panic that went through Kingston's nearly seven-foot-tall body when he walked into the kitchen of the Keep and saw his mate lying on the floor.

Her tawny skin was pale and cold to the touch. Eyes shut, body limp, he picked her up and rushed her down the hall to their rooms. The suite had been his since he'd moved in a few decades ago, but it was theirs now.

He might have been mated to Neela, but the she-Dragon had never shared his bed nor any of the rooms in his suite. He still felt pangs of regret when he thought of her, but he knew where he belonged now.

There was only room for Holley in his heart and, for the moment, in his mind. He'd expected his beast to calm after mating her the previous night, but he'd been wrong. The Dragon wanted her even more.

It was difficult to leave her in bed that morning while he went with his team to investigate a lead, they had on the now banned group of Loyalists who had followed their evil leader down a path from which no redemption could be had. Murder, kidnapping, mind-rape, and more counts of heinous crimes than he cared to contemplate could be laid at their door.

Those scumbags needed to be found. Offner most of all. The *sonovabitch* had no morals to speak of. What Warlock did?

He'd sold his soul, broken his oath to magic and to the supernatural world, and now, he would reap the benefits of what he sowed. With any luck, that would be at Kingston's hands or claws.

Claws, huffed his Dragon.

Still, none of that mattered at the moment. Holley's breathing was shallow and her skin like ice. Kingston roared and Egros came running. After the

Witch took one look at her, he consulted with Byram, and both were clueless how to help her.

"It's like she's in a coma," Egros explained, "a magical one, but not as bad as before. I think you can reverse it, Kingston."

"You mean, I have to bite her?"

"Yes," Byram nodded.

"Leave us," he commanded.

The Witch and Vampire did as he asked, closing the door behind them. The first time he'd bitten her there had been curiosity and attraction, perhaps even a sense of destiny. The second time, there'd been pleasure and an urgency of need that was indescribable. This time there was something else. Something he'd been too afraid to say aloud.

"Holley! Holley, I am sorry this will hurt you, my love, but I don't know what else to do," he pulled her sweater off her body, not wanting to ruin it.

She loved getting new, modern clothes. It was something about the way material from this time felt against her skin. He inhaled a breath to steady himself and placed the shirt beside her, leaving her torso clothed in a simple camisole. His Witch still hated underthings, he acknowledged with a concerned quirk of his lips.

Kingston lifted her in his embrace. He brushed

her hair away from her face and neck, carefully, methodically, until he could place his teeth over the scar of his mating mark. Then he bit.

Holley jerked in his arms before he had time to seal them properly, but she was okay! His Dragon's heart soared with love for her as she shivered against him and opened dazed green eyes to his. After that, it was only a matter of seconds before he was kissing her.

"Is it too much," he growled as he tugged off clothes and shoes, grinning when he checked to see what color dragon she was wearing on her feet today.

Pale pink. Today she was wearing pink dragons. His beast huffed in indignance, but Kingston thought she was positively adorable.

"Never too much. Please, I need you," she moaned into his mouth, dueling her tongue cleverly with his until he was the one gasping for air.

His cock throbbed in his jeans and before he could properly remove them, his claws popped free and Kingston shredded the fuckers off his body. The scent of his mate's arousal was delicious. It filled the room, whetting his appetite and coaxing his beast to the forefront.

Mine. Mate. Claim.

His Dragon hissed and scratched. He didn't fully

understand, but who was he to question. The woman was claimed three times over, but still the creature demanded more.

"Want to taste you, sweet," he growled and laid her down on her back.

Holley moaned, eyes glazed with lust as he ran his hands down the length of her body. His palms heated her still-chilled flesh, and she arched up to get closer to him, seeming to want more of his careful attentions. Her breasts swelled with her arousal and her nipples hardened into tiny little berries he could not wait to sample.

Kingston closed his lips over one, tugging it with his teeth until she moaned his name. Holley pulled his hair, pushing her chest more fully into his mouth. Fuck, she was so hot when she was demanding.

He treated her other perfect breast to more of the same, running his hands down to her hips and thighs. He spread them wide, finding her uncovered pussy with determined fingers.

"You're so wet, so tight," he growled as he stroked the pad of his thumb over her small bundle of nerves, tempting her to madness while he stretched her channel with his other thick digits.

He caught each one of Holley's throaty moans with his mouth and savored them as he kissed her. It was almost enough to make him come right there, but the beast inside demanded more.

Kingston abandoned her breasts and mouth in search of other treats located further down the wonderland that was her body. Anticipation had precum beading on the head of his cock. He reached down and squeezed his shaft, rubbing that pearl up and down his length, before using both hands to smooth the silky skin of her luscious thighs. She trembled beneath his touch, flexing her hips instinctively, seeking his attention.

She had it. Completely. Now that she was warm, her tawny complexion glowed like bronze in the soft light coming from the fireplace. Funny, that wasn't his doing, but whatever. The Keep had a lot of explaining to do, and perhaps this was an act of contrition.

He used his shoulders to widen her legs and licked his lips at the display before him. She was so perfect. Glistening with her arousal, Kingston could not wait to lap at her honey. And he didn't. He bent his head and swiped his tongue along her lips.

"Oh gods," she moaned and clutched at the blankets beneath her, but he was only getting started.

Slow and steady, with strokes of his long, and sometimes forked, tongue, Kingston made love to his mate with his mouth. He tapped his finger against her clit while he drove into her sweet, hot, sheath. Tasting her deeply for the first time and drinking her down.

She was better than wine, better than anything he ever had. He was high on his love for her. Intoxicated and bespelled by his sweet Witch. Holley lifted up, pressing herself to him, and he allowed it.

Fuck that. He fucking loved it. He traded his tongue for fingers and returned his attention on her tight little clit. That nubbin was his ticket to making his mate come harder than ever before.

He growled deep in his throat, the sound making a vibrator of his now-forked-tongue as he delivered a myriad of circles, swirls, and taps to the sensitive little bundle of nerves.

Suck, swirl, tap, suck, swirl, tap, tap, tap.

"Oh gods!"

Fuck, she was gorgeous. And his. All his. His Dragon insisted he remember that even as he gripped her hip with his free hand and felt his claws dig into the flesh there, leaving a scratch that would mark her again, same as his bite.

She did not seem to mind. In fact, she pressed deeper against him. Pushing her sweet pussy into his mouth she groaned loudly and covered his hand with hers. Like she knew he was marking her again, and even more wondrous, she wanted it. Holley bucked against him and clutched his hair, but he was relentless.

Pleasuring her was the only goal he had at the moment. And it was goddamn important. He felt the first spasms ripple through her as more moisture gushed forward.

His Dragon growled with pride. She was his. He was going to make her come again, this time on his cock, then he would claim her once more.

Determination set him on fire and Kingston doubled his efforts, licking, sucking, and fucking her with his fingers and tongue until she arched up in a soundless scream that echoed through his heart.

Mine!

He moved up her body before the tremors of her first orgasm could stop and plunged into her silky hot depths. Her sex squeezed his cock like a velvet vise and she wrapped her legs around his waist, encouraging him to move.

"Yes, now, now, now," she begged and who was he to deny her.

Never that. He could only give her pleasure. It was in his fucking DNA. She was the light of his life, his fire, his reason.

"I love you," he said stopping suddenly as the realization came crashing down into reality.

Holley's mossy eyes smiled up at him, though her mouth was serious. She held his face between her small hands and pulled him down to kiss her lips gently.

"I know, mate, I love you too," she returned and Kingston moved deep within her.

So slowly. So very slowly, he thought he would die or maybe kill them both, from the sheer amount of pleasure alone.

She was precious to him, and he would cherish her always. He was her shield. Her protector against all things. Her fated mate. Her Diamond Dragon.

Mine.

His hands held her close as he pushed inside of her welcoming body. The two of them moaned in unison, a symphonic sound that reverberated in the room.

Holley's eyes never left his as they kissed and touched. It was more than bodies, he realized, she was touching his soul. Caressing him so deeply and permanently, he would never be the same. Fuck, he never wanted to be.

"I love you," he whispered once more and

brushed his nose against hers while he rotated his hips in tight, slow, circles.

"I love you," he said it again and kissed her lower lip, tugging it between his teeth as he slid his long legs against her smooth ones, grinding his pubis into her pussy, and dragging a husky moan from her mouth.

His Dragon was wild for her. The legendary beast completely infatuated with his mate, his maiden fair, his one and only.

"I love you," he increased pace, fucking her harder and faster and watching her expression for the right moment to strike.

"Kingston, now," she yelled, and he struck like lightning, biting her once more, marking her flesh, this time above her breast.

He clung to her while Holley's orgasm rippled around him, then Kingston roared with pain-tinted pleasure. Rearing up, he saw his mate's eyes go white as she chanted something unintelligible, something magical.

His own orgasm erupted from him like a long-awaited volcano and he cried out her name as he coated her walls with his cum. Fucking hell, the searing pain finally receded giving way to pure pleasure, though where it had occurred, there remained a dull ache.

When he could move again, Kingston opened his eyes and looked down. Holly was still catching her breath. Her arms were limp above her head, and he kissed her cheek and cradled her close. Then he turned and looked at his bicep. There, like a brand, was a marking. Like a tattoo.

Claimed, his Dragon exhaled a puff of smoke and for the first time ever, his beast was truly at peace.

"I am sorry if that hurt you," she said breathlessly, "I suppose I got carried away."

"It's alright, love," he smiled wide, unable to hide the joy that was bursting from his heart.

Diamond Dragons had notoriously tough hides, even in their human form. No doubt, she had to put a little extra into whatever spell she'd conjured to mark him as hers. He looked down at the angry red marking and smiled. It was a shield with a heart inside it, surrounded by flames.

"I love it and you," he said and meant every word.

"I love you too," she replied sleepily before nodding off.

This time he would stay until she awakened.

Chapter Thirteen

"So, what are we cooking today?" Holley inquired.

"Well, in exchange for you teaching me how to make that wonderful skin salve you gave me last week, I thought I would teach you how to make pizza," Fergie clapped.

"*You* will be teaching her?' snorted her best friend, Jessenia and even Holley laughed at that.

"Fine, you will be learning from a certain haughty little kitchen bitch I know."

Holley laughed as the two women continued to tease each other while she started to gather ingredients from the cabinets. The last few days had gone by rather smoothly and she was happy to have some time with the females.

Mostly, she used what was on hand and was incredibly surprised at how rapidly she could order what were once very rare ingredients. Some common sage, local honey, a little lavender, virgin olive oil, and some chamomile flowers made for a very nice salve indeed.

Her mind wandered to Kingston. The man was absolutely wonderful, but she knew he was neglecting his duties to care for her. Last night, she'd assured him that she could stay home without incident. After all, being mated to a Guardian was not for the faint of heart. She did not want him to think she was a hinderance to his vows. He swore an oath to protect magic and she would not be the reason he broke it.

The sound of voices in the living room brought all three female heads whipping around. Holley frowned. She knew from the properly chastised Keep that not everyone was happy she was there. it was something she'd brushed aside, until now. Truth was, it hurt to think one of them saw her as an interloper.

"I don't understand what the fuck he is doing in there with her," growled voices from inside the living room.

"Dude, easy. That's his mate."

"Neela was his mate," insisted the former.

"That was different, cump, he already explained it-"

"Nah man, fuck that. If we can just go around picking and choosing what vows to honor then why are we even here?"

"The fuck did you say?"

The sounds of blows being exchanged and furniture crashing into walls brought Holley, Fergie, and Jessenia, who'd been something of a constant fixture since the unfortunate incident in the kitchen, running. Furio and Storm were locked together in what kind of looked like a hug, but Holley had the good sense to know was a fierce battle.

"Stop it!" yelled Fergie.

"Guys, come on!"

"This is because of me isn't it? Enough!" Holley bit her lip and watched the two friends pound each other into the floor.

"No, it's just," Jessenia hedged, but Holley knew it was true.

She was the cause of the rift between the men. Furio was the sole sour face at every meal and gathering since the beginning. Apparently, the Stallion Shifter held Neela in such high esteem that he did not believe she could or should be replaced.

Even after Kingston had come clean about the truth of his relationship between the she-Dragon and himself, the stubborn Draft Horse Shifter refused to accept Holley! He actually believed she was wrong somehow. Holley's heart ached for the man. From what she knew from her years in the manse's hollows, he was orphaned at a tender age.

With no real family of his own, Furio had made one out of his group of Guardians. With Neela as the maternal figurehead, he felt betrayed by Kingston's actions and Holley's very existence. But that was no excuse to break the damn furniture! She growled and called on her magic.

"I said, enough!" she yelled and her voice echoed off the walls, full of her power.

The two men immediately split apart from one another and were held suspended over the broken remnants of the sofa. Annoyance coursed through her at the mess and she gave them a shake with just a nod.

"Hey!"

"Ow," growled Storm whose teeth had knocked together at the last little jiggle.

"Look at you, two grown men behaving like children"

"Sorry, Holley," growled the Wolf, but Furio refused to look at her.

"Are you finished now? Ready to act like men and not boys?"

Displeasure dripped from every word as she watched the men look at each other than back at the very angry little Witch. Storm nodded.

"Good," she said and with another nod dropped them both on the floor, "start by cleaning this mess. Then I think you will both benefit from time in the garden."

The small fenced in garden just off the kitchen was Holley's pride and joy. Kingston had made a sort of gift of it and presented it to her just the other morning. Apparently, he had some of the guys clean out all the old vegetation. They even tilled the soil despite it being winter to ready it for planting in the spring.

She'd ordered heavy ceramic pots and large wooden boxes that still needed to be put together. All of that from the computer. She could not wait to see it in bloom. Shopping was one of her new favorite pastimes.

Well, second favorite.

And shopping online meant she never even had to leave the house! While that was certainly marvelous, she did enjoy going to town. But she only ever went with Kingston. Her mate was somewhat protective of her, which she secretly loved.

The crates she'd ordered, along with special seeds and fertilizers, would hold herbs and roots off the ground for easy access. She'd already begun to plan for the upcoming season and had even asked Jessenia's input on several occasions.

"Shit, I mean, okay, okay, I can move some stuff for you," growled Storm, but the second he stood he went to embrace his worried looking mate who growled at Furio.

"I'm not working in no garden," he finger-combed his hair back into its ponytail and stomped away from her.

"Fine, then you can clean in here," she called after him, "you broke it, you clean it, or you will both be eating pickled eggs and sardines for every meal for the next two months."

Storm paled and a sound that was suspiciously like a whinny came from the direction Furio had gone in. Holley turned her back on them and went to the kitchen with Jessenia following behind.

"He doesn't mean it," she drawled, "I mean, Furio is the nicest of the bunch. Always light-hearted and laughing. He was the one who was nicest to Fergie when she first mated Storm. I am so sorry."

"It is not your doing," Holley wiped her face.

She felt foolish for crying, but she couldn't help it. An outcast most her life, it was a familiar though unwelcome feeling to be unwanted. One she wished she could forget.

"Do you think I could show you how to make the salve later?"

"Sure, I'll go ahead and prep the dough and everything for the pizzas. You can help put them together, yeah?"

"That sounds divine," she squeezed Jessenia's arm and walked outside.

The garden gate was newly fixed. The shiny, black wrought-iron gleamed in the morning sun despite it being late November. Holley simply loved the look of.

It was chilly outside, but she relished the cold breeze as it whipped her hair around her shoulders and molded her long skirt to her legs. Fergie had tried to get her to wear something called leggings, but they were stockings for sure!

She was not about to walk outdoors like that. Kingston had pointed out that her penchant for going out without underwear was a tad more risqué, but she wouldn't budge. They compromised on the whole underwear thing anyway. The other day, he took her shopping and she found something called boxer briefs which were wonderfully comfortable and covered her completely.

Whenever he was not home, she promised to wear one of the six dozen pairs he'd bought her beneath her skirts. And when he was home, well, then it was up to him to find out, wasn't it?

The gate was open when she got there, but Holley was too lost in thoughts about her Dragon that she didn't stop to think that anything was amiss. The sound of the gate door banging shut brought her head up sharp and fast.

"You!"

Fright filled her, and she stepped back, but something, or rather, someone grabbed her from behind. Holley struggled against the offensive hold. Her foul-smelling captor struck her across the head, then proceeded to lick her cheek.

The urge to vomit welled up inside of her, but Holley found herself unable to move. The creature holding her hissed, and she recalled Fergie's debacle with the heinous Gila Shifters whose saliva was laced with venom.

"I see time has not changed you, heathen-spawn," growled the familiar though time-ravaged man.

A man she'd never expected to see again. He stalked towards her, leaning heavily on a cane for support and his pockmarked skin seemed to drip and melt before her eyes. Beneath was even more hideous disfigurement. As gruesome and gory an image as she had ever seen.

"I have found you now, and with you, this place. For hundreds of years I searched, waiting, but the magic wards that kept you hidden, also hid the castle from prying eyes. I bet you didn't know that did you? Ha!" the man she knew as Preacher Milton cackled briefly before black spittle ran down his chin.

"At last, I will seize control, and you my dear, are the means that I will use to take my rightful place at the center of all magic!"

She could barely believe her eyes. The man she had known was a religious fanatic at best, but this man was something else. In fact, he was not a man at all. She smelled magic rolling off him, but it was tainted.

Putrid and rotting, the stink stung her eyes even more than the wind. She tried to whimper, but the sound would not come. Still immobile due to the Gila's venom, Holley was helpless to respond.

She could only stare in horror, eyes tearing against the cold, as the Gila Shifter lifted her onto his shoulder and carried her out of the garden to the cellar stairs behind the Keep.

Kingston, she thought, *where are you?*

Chapter Fourteen

Kingston's enormous white Diamond Dragon soared beneath the darkening clouds as he neared the Keep. The day's hunt had gone fairly well. They'd found the nest where Offner's Loyalist scum had been hiding the foul Warlock, but of course he was nowhere to be seen.

After dropping off the small Lounge of Gila Shifters they'd rounded up at the Enforcers' compound, he decided to let Byram handle the paperwork and took to the skies. He'd had to work to retract his claws and fangs while handling the criminals.

His beast wanted out. He wanted his mate, and so did he for that matter. The little Witch with the pale eyes and tawny skin was all he thought about. He found heaven in her touch, bliss in her arms, sweetness in her kiss. But it was so much more than that too.

Who knew Dragons were such romantics? But it was true. The Witch was his mate. His everything. He wanted to bathe in her scent. To be in her presence all the time. No matter how impractical. A point she'd made last night in between kissing him silly and loving him until he saw stars.

Kingston flapped his enormous wings harder and faster, using his aerodynamic shape to allow the wind speed him along. He caught sight of the Keep in the distance, hiding among the pines and shrubs of the great New Jersey Barrens.

Odd, he thought as his keen Dragon eyes caught something off about the manse. It was as if the building itself was beckoning him home faster, calling to him as it never had before. Something was wrong.

He searched inside of himself for the *matebond* that connected him to Holley, but it was barely glowing. Kingston opened his jaws and shot a stream of flame into the quickly darkening skies. Lightning flashed overhead and thunder rolled loudly, echoing his growing rage.

Whatever the problem, Kingston was willing to settle it with claws and fire. Dragon fire to be precise. Willing himself to calm, it was no easy feat.

Something primal and not quite tame inside him reared up at the thought of his mate in danger. He had no proof, only this feeling in his gut and it wouldn't let up.

His Dragon's cry echoed through the Pine Barrens, bringing all the Guardians in residence, and their mates and friends, to the backyard where the garden gate was swinging madly in the breeze. He took a deep inhale and snarled.

Something foul had passed that way. Something not entirely human. And the soon-to-be-dead-motherfucker had his mate.

Roooooooaaaaaaarrrr!

"Fuck!"

"Kingston, what is it?"

Summoning as much restraint as he could, Kingston shifted to his human form, catching the pair of sweats someone tossed his way and shrugging them on even as he used his Dragon's eyes to search the grounds. She was there roughly twenty minutes ago he judged from the fading scent. And she wasn't alone.

"Where'd he get that ink?" he heard one of them

ask and snapped his head to look at the Shifter who spoke.

Furio. His fastest and at one time most dependable Guardian. The Stallion had not been himself lately. Looking at him now, in this agitated state, Kingston was stunned to see him clearly for the first time.

"Holy shit, *cump*," the man pointed, and he looked down.

His torso was covered in whirling flames of orange and yellow. White smoke billowed upward and little sparkling lights zipping around him. He growled with a start, but it was his added powers. Those he'd gotten as a result of finding and mating with his *conpar*.

"Uh, you're on fire, boss," Storm added unnecessarily.

He ignored the stares and whispers. Holley needed him to focus.

"When was the last time any of you spoke with Holley?" he growled in a voice so thick with his Dragon he was barely discernible.

"Uh, we were going to make pizza and she was going to show us how to make a salve," Jessenia piped in.

"But Storm and I had a disagreement," Furio bowed his head.

His feelings were like a beacon to Kingston, who as his Alpha and the leader of their team wanted to offer comfort to the man. However, seeing as how his actions had put Kingston's own mate in harm's way, he also wanted to rip him a new asshole.

But his primary goal was to find Holley. Still, regret and emotions poured from Furio into him and he did the only thing he could, he nodded at the man, Acknowledging his repentance and he was glad for it. It was the only thing that saved him from being charred to a crisp by his angry as fuck Dragon who wanted his mate back now.

"The women came in and Holley, well" his lips quirked and Kingston acknowledged it as a sign the Draft Horse Shifter respected his mate, his Dragon growled softly in approval, "she kicked our asses, boss. Took us to task like a pro and made us clean up our shit."

"Yeah, then I, uh, took Storm inside to check him over for injury," Fergie cleared her throat which left the rest up to interpretation.

"She was going outside to clear her head I think," Jessenia added.

"You let her go alone?" he turned to the kitchen Witch, but Furio moved in front of her.

"It's my fault. She asked me to work in the garden and I refused. She was outside alone because of me."

"It was a lot of things, not just him," Jessenia's voice rose as she tried to push her way in front of Furio.

Clearly, something was going on between the two of them, but Kingston did not care. Not then. He closed his eyes searching for her scent and started to move.

"Listen up," he growled to everyone there, "Holley is my mate. This 'ink' is her mating mark, I can feel her inside the Keep. The spirits, the *mane-tuwak* are watching but they can't interfere," he said as if caught in some kind of live feed he was getting from the manse itself.

"Can you find her?"

"Yes, I think so."

"Well, what are you all waiting for?" Fergie bent down and picked up one of the spades from the ground, "let's get those fuckers!"

He raised his eyebrow as Jessenia reached into her back pocket and pulled out a small vial. She nodded at Fergie and moved to stand beside her and Storm.

"What? It's an attack spell. Don't worry, Holley showed me what to use," she smirked.

Kingston's hearts welled with pride at the men and women before him. They were willing to risk their lives for his mate.

"Thank you, but I don't think you should all follow me. What if it's a trap? I need someone to stay here," he began.

"No way."

"We're coming-"

"Listen up! I will go with Kingston," Furio stated.

Kingston felt his Guardian's inside of him as he never had before. Their thoughts and feelings projected like a newsreel. Storm's brow was furrowed in worry as he considered bringing his mate back within range of Offner and his vile henchmen. Fergie was frightened, especially because she had a secret. A baby, he thought in wonder and sent waves of calm to the couple.

"You three stay here," Furio pointed at them.

"No way, Buster!" Fergie growled, but Jessenia interrupted her.

"It's better this way Ferg. You guys stay and the

three of us will go. Egros, Elena, and Byram should be here any minute. You can send them after us."

"Darn it," she stomped her stiletto on the ground.

"He's right, *conpar*, we will watch their rear and make sure no more men follow them," Storm wrapped his arms around her and pulled her back against him.

Kingston nodded at the Wolf and turned to where Furio and Jessenia were pointedly not looking at each other.

"Come on, we wasted too much time already," he growled and took off around the back of the Keep to where a pair of cellar doors flapped in the chilled breeze.

At that moment, rain began to pour down and lightning flashed once more, hitting close to where he stood. The entire fucking earth could flood and he wouldn't care, not unless he had Holley back in his arms.

Rrrrrrroooooaaaaarrrrrrr!

"Where does that lead?' Jessenia called over the rising storm.

"The furnace room," he growled and took off down the stairs and into the darkness, following the stench of the rot and death, and beneath it blueberries.

Mine.

There was no light but, Kingston was able to see using his Dragon's eyes. Think infrared but without the goggles. He inhaled deeply, wishing he had some of Storm's strength of smell, but for what it was worth, it was like he was seeing in 4D.

Furio grabbed onto Jessenia when the Witch stumbled in the dark and Kingston raised a finger to his lips. They were getting closer. He wanted to use his new powers but hesitated. The last thing he needed was to rush in and put Holley in even more danger.

It wasn't the stink of the Gila Shifters or of Offner himself that told him they were closing in on the men who had his mate. No, it was the pulsing little sparks of light that were zipping all around and practically pulling him forward.

He felt as if his entire body was buzzing with energy. Then he felt her. The first thing he saw was the broken wall where Jessenia and Fergie had accidentally tried to drill to install an ethernet cable.

But this time his mate was not laid out like some sacrifice, trapped and suspended alone by a spell only he could break. Like some modern-day Snow White.

No. This time there were three Gila fuckers

holding her down while the mad Warlock Offner recited an incantation in *Demonspeak.* The guttural sounds were harsh to his Dragon's ears and the foul stench they pulled forth from the crack in the floor was polluted and tainted.

Kingston's body began to Shift, but it was too small for a full-sized Dragon. Using his extreme Alpha powers, he did a half -Shift, something only the strongest Shifters with supreme control and balance of their dual natures could manage to pull off.

Yes, he was enraged, but this was his best chance to save her unscathed. The beast recognized that and did not fight him as he called his white, diamond-shaped scales to cover his arms, shoulders and chest. Horns erupted from his forehead, while his fangs descended, and claws popped free of his fingers.

Kingston's skin became pale as alabaster and wings protruded from his back, as well as a spiked tail. In this shape he could breathe fire, and block against just about any weapon known to man or supe.

He moved forward stealthily, in time with the spirits of the Keep. As if sensing his presence and intent, the manse's *manetuwak* seemed to come to a decision. They accepted him, hiding him in the shadows until it was the right time to pounce.

Like right when that evil sonovabitch held an athame over his beautiful mate's face.

Motherfucker. With a roar so loud the basement shook, Kingston emerged. His body was shrouded in spiraling flames as he shot a stream of fire out of his mouth, hitting the first fucker he saw. Furio and Jessenia got to work against the others as he circled his nemesis.

"You are too late! My master comes for the Witch," hissed Offner.

His eyes met Holley's and all of his protective instinct and his beast's rage burst forth.

"Then he shall die with you," promised Kingston.

Chapter Fifteen

"You will die this time, I shall see to it," Preacher Milton, whom she suspected was the Warlock Offner all along, hissed at her.

With a nod of his wrinkled, misshapen head, his Gila minion slapped her cheek hard. Still immobile from the venom, Holley was seriously getting angry. She closed her eyes and sifted through the layers of bindings looking for a way out.

The bastard had learned a lot about magic since they'd last met. No wonder, what with him being a Warlock now and all. The Demon had given him power for which he of course bargained his soul.

A hefty payment, she thought with disdain.

"You shall not win this time! I will kill you and seize control of your magic. I shall pay my debt to the

Demon with your blood," he cackled as his monsters held her down.

From her position half off the stone slab, she could see a crack in the foundation of the Keep. The *manetuwak* was trying to defend her, but it could not heal itself and keep her alive at the same time.

"That is not going to work. You should know that Warlock," she said from stiff lips.

"I will steal your magic from your dying soul before it leaves your body and feed it to the Demon. Then I will plunge this vein myself and reap the benefits of eons of magical energy."

"Doesn't matter if you kill me," she gasped weakly as he continued to siphon her life's force with his evil spell, "the Keep will have my powers. It's part of our bargain. You have to give for what you take in magic as in everything," she smiled weakly and was stunned to realize the venom was wearing off.

"You're wrong," the crazed preacher raised a sharp dagger and Holley tried to gather her energy to move away, but those Gila Shifters were just too strong.

This was not her end. She could hardly accept it as such. Captive for centuries to have emerged for what? So this bastard could steal her life and her love from her?

"Ahh, no," she yelled as her mate emerged from the shadows.

"NO!" Kingston attacked, shooting fire at one of her captors before turning on the Warlock.

That was fine. She was able to hit one of them with her magic while Furio and Jessenia took care of the other. She slid off the table and hit the floor, but not before the bastard's eyes caught hers.

"I have you now, Offner, yield," growled Kingston, magnificent in his half-shift.

"You might have cornered me, Dragon, but I have one play left," he threw the blade at her, but before Kingston could lunge for it, the man had his claws out and was chanting dark magic to weave around his body.

Holley cried out as the knife pierced her stomach. She slumped sightlessly against the stone floor. No, this could not be happening, she moaned as Kingston howled in fury. But the Warlock was not done. Even as he chanted, his body morphed and swelled in the small room.

Black, stinking skin bubbled with poisonous ooze as his gnarled claws struck out to attack. The scent of Kingston's blood as the bastard struck his thigh invaded her senses and Holley yelled for him to watch out.

Time seemed to stand still for a moment as pain filled her. She held his gaze and nodded. Kingston would want to go to her, but he needed to end Offner first.

"Get him" she commanded and her mate roared mightily shaking the room with his rage.

Flames engulfed his body as he turned and grabbed for the Warlock's disgusting form. His claws shredded his diseased skin, but he kept on pulling him closer in a fierce farce of a hug. Offner howled, but Kingston was relentless.

He pulled his magic to him and called on his Dragon's fire to burn the oath-breaker until there was nothing but charred bone. Suddenly a guttural roar sounded from the ether and Kingston turned and hurled the dusty corpse into the maw of the Demon who'd claimed Offner's tainted soul.

That evil had no purchase in that mortal world with oath-breaker dead, and after closing his jaws over the dead remains of the evil man she knew as Milton, the Demon went back to hell. Leaving Furio and Jessenia with two Gila Shifters bound and gagged on the floor. And Kingston, her sweet mate, sucking in air as he recovered from the battle.

He was a mighty warrior indeed, she thought even as her spirit began to leave her physical shape. The pain she'd felt was inconsequential as rivulets of blood flowed from her wound.

Damn it, she groaned. It was her heart that was breaking now. Seeing him one last time meant the world, but she didn't want to leave. Kingston ran to her side, losing hold of his Dragon as he did so.

"Holley! Holley!" he roared and shook her, gathering her in his arms.

His body trembled as he sobbed openly, pleading with her to return to him. She wanted to. Oh gods, how she wanted to.

The cold shadows of the veil beckoned her forth and she tried to slow her pace, but it was no good. She was dying.

"No," a voice said, *"you must go back to him, make him happy."*

The shape of a lovely blonde she-Dragon came into view. With the beauty was the spitting image of Kingston, only this Dragon was platinum blonde and blue-eyed. His grin was the same as he held the woman's ghostly hand in his.

"I am Edgar, sweet sister, and it is my pleasure to meet you. Go back now. Tell Kingston to be happy, for us. And remind the Keep every now and then to honor their deal. The others are watching," he added facetiously.

Holley nodded. She could not speak, but she felt their peace and good will flow through her like a thousand wishes and dreams. She rushed back to herself and inhaled a great gulp of air back into her lungs.

"Holley! Thank the gods, thank the gods," Kingston gripped her tighter, kissing her face and hair. "What do you need? Tell me, please, anything at all. I will get it for you," he sniffed, wiping at his tear-stained cheeks and nose.

He'd never looked more beautiful to her. Holley cupped his face in her hands and marveled at his fierce, unwavering devotion.

"You. I only need you."

Epilogue

"Are you shittin' me?" Furio snorted and dropped the piece of broccolini he was munching on back onto his plate.

The entire group was in heaven with the superb meals the *manetuwak* made for them. With a fully stocked kitchen, the Guardians and their mates, *and guests*, were more than happy to resume their duties, respectful of their sacred responsibility to the spirits of the manse.

A happy Keep meant happy Guardians. And that meant "cutlet time" as Holley was fond of saying after binge-watching several seasons of *Jersey Shore*. She was familiar enough with modern terminology, but every now and then there was a phrase that threw her. Like the one Furio just uttered.

"What does that even mean? Does one shit on one or near one?" Holley inquired and Kingston choked on a bite of the savory chicken dish Jessenia had cooked up.

"Nice," Jessenia said and shook her head.

"At any rate, Furio, I am not shitting on anyone. The fact is, the Keep was built on a very powerful ley line that was sacred to my father's people and known to the *supernaturals* who commissioned this place to be built."

"Were they Guardians?" asked Storm.

"Yes, and no," she took a bite of the chicken and moaned in delight.

Jessenia had lost the rental she and Fergie had together and because she was always there anyway, Holley had invited her to move in. She was not a Guardian, but she was quickly becoming family.

The Witch smiled around the room and sighed to herself. They were already a family indeed.

"Well, who were they then?" Elena chimed in.

"From what the *manetuwak* told me, they were Guardians of Chaos, and Enforcers too, and also a few local Witches and Shifter groups. You see each had claim to the land, but they knew it was being targeted. They built this place to protect it."

"Really?"

"Yes, I suppose they weren't counting on the Keep having a personality of its own," she smirked and the lights flashed.

"We thought it was all you," Fergie grinned.

"Well, I communicate with the spirits, but I don't control them."

"Magic isn't meant to be controlled," Kingston added and her gaze met his.

"Indeed, it is not," she agreed.

Later that night, wrapped in the arms of the man she loved more than her own life, Holley sighed contentedly.

"What are you thinking about?" his husky voice broke the serenity, but she remained peaceful, secure in the warmth of his love.

"I was thinking about the first time I saw you."

"When I bit you?"

"Oh no. It was decades before that. You were so serious, so set in your ways."

"You knew," he lifted his head and what she saw in his eyes made her heart swell, "You knew for all that time?"

"Yes," she said because lying to him would never be an option.

"I am so sorry," he held her tight and she smiled.

"I am not. It gave me time to know you. Time to observe you unnoticed. I fell in love with you like that, Kingston. Fated mates or not, I have loved you for many lifetimes," she reached up and kissed him.

Savoring the feel of his lips as they opened and his tongue swirled around hers. Holley moaned and moved until she was astride the big man. Lifting her body, she slid along his shaft and accepted Kingston's hard length deep inside of her.

"Holley," he growled, hands on her hips as he guided her into a frenzy of motion and passion unlike any.

Each time better than the last. And this was only the beginning, or so he kept telling her. So far, it was true. He thrust upwards, in time with her downward swivels. Each repeated motion sent shards of bliss exploding along her spine throughout every fiber of her being. Her magic closed in around them, wrapping them in a blanket where his Dragon met her powers.

Together they reached untold heights. The ecstasy she found in his arms was pure heaven. Heart near to bursting with love, she moaned his name as her pleasure reached its pinnacle with Kingston right there with her.

"I love you, *conpar*," he growled softly into her hair and she loved his fascination with it.

She always found the most intense pleasure in the way he loved her. And she knew he did down to her marrow. It was in the way his golden eyes caressed her like hands, the way his lips seemed to smile whenever she was around. Yes, they were good for one another.

"I love you too," she replied hugging him tight to her breast.

Holley never had to fear the cold again. Not with her Dragon Shield to keep her warm and safe from harm. He would protect her always. She trusted that with all her soul, and whether he knew it or not, she would do the same for him.

That is what it meant to be mated to a Guardian of Chaos. Together they were stronger, better, and more powerful than anything else.

Loving him was easy, getting his love in return was a bonus.

Give for what you take, she thought as sleep came easily to her now.

"Mate."

. . .

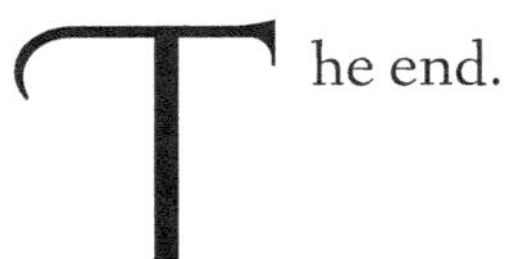

he end.

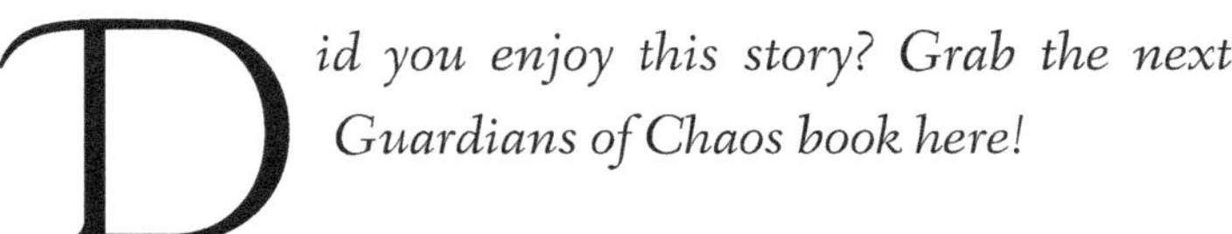

id you enjoy this story? Grab the next *Guardians of Chaos* book here!

P.S

Don't forget to tell me how you liked this story by leaving your honest review! *No pressure.* 😉

A review can be one or two brief sentences where you simply state whether you enjoyed the story and would recommend it to someone! It is an enormous help to authors and the best way for us to reach larger audiences so we can keep writing the stories you love!

Thank you so much!

Xoxo!

Del mare alla stella,

C.D. Gorri

Have you met my Dragons?

The Falk Clan Tales are my stories surrounding four Dragon Shifter brothers and how they find their one true mates.

Each brother's chest is marked with his rose, the magical link to his heart and his magic. They each have a matching gemstone to go with it.

She's given up on love, but he's just begun.

In *The Dragon's Valentine* we meet the eldest Falk brother, Callius. He is on a mission to find a Castle and his one true mate, one he can trust with his diamond rose....

His heart is frozen; can she change his mind about love?

In *The Dragon's Christmas Gift* our attention shifts to Alexsander, the youngest brother of the four. He has resigned himself to a life alone, until he meets *her.*

Some wounds run deep, can a Dragon's heart be unbroken?

The Dragon's Heart is the story of Edric Falk who has vowed never to love again, but that changes when he meets his feisty mate, Joselyn Curacao.

She just wants a little fun, he's looking for a lifetime.

We finally meet Nikolai Falk and his sexy Shifter mate in *The Dragon's Secret.*

Now available in a boxed set.

Look for The Dragon's Treasure in 2022!

Connect with C.D. Gorri

To learn more about me please visit:

    https://www.cdgorri.com

    https://www.facebook.com/Cdgorribooks

    https://twitter.com/cgor22

    https://www.bookbub.com/authors/c-d-gorri

TikTok

Visit my website to find out more about my supernatural world also known as the Grazi Kelly Universe and sign up to be a subscriber!

    https://www.cdgorri.com/newsletter

Have you met my Bears?

Looking for a Paranormal Romance series that is loads of growly fun?

Meet the Barvale Clan first in the Bear Claw Tales! A complete shifter romance series about 4 brothers who discover and need to win their fated mates!

Followed by two more spin off series, the Barvale Clan Tales and the Barvale Holiday Tales!

No cliffhangers. Steamy PNR fun. Go and read your next happily ever after today!

Other Titles by C.D. Gorri

Other Titles by C.D. Gorri

Young Adult Urban Fantasy Books:

Wolf Moon: A Grazi Kelly Novel Book 1

Hunter Moon: A Grazi Kelly Novel Book 2

Rebel Moon: A Grazi Kelly Novel Book 3

Winter Moon: A Grazi Kelly Novel Book 4

Chasing The Moon: A Grazi Kelly Short 5

Blood Moon: A Grazi Kelly Novel 6

*Get all 6 books NOW AVAILABLE IN A BOXED SET:

The Complete Grazi Kelly Novel Series

Casting Magic: The Angela Tanner Files 1

Keeping Magic: The Angela Tanner Files 2

G'Witches Magical Mysteries Series

Co-written with P. Mattern

G'Witches

G'Witches 2: The Hary Harbinger

Home for the Howlidays: A Macconwood Pack Tale 6

A Silver Wedding: A Macconwood Pack Tale 7

Mine Furever: A Macconwood Pack Tale 8

A Furry Little Christmas: A Macconwood Pack Tale 9

Also available in two boxed sets:

The Macconwood Pack Tales Volume 1

Shifters Furever: The Macconwood Pack Tales Volume 2

The Falk Clan Tales:

The Dragon's Valentine: A Falk Clan Novel 1

The Dragon's Christmas Gift: A Falk Clan Novel 2

The Dragon's Heart: A Falk Clan Novel 3

The Dragon's Secret: A Falk Clan Novel 4

The Dragon's Treasure: A Falk Clan Novel 5

Dragon Mates: The Falk Clan Complete Series Boxed Set Books 1-4

The Bear Claw Tales:

Bearly Breathing: A Bear Claw Tale 1

Bearly There: A Bear Claw Tale 2

Bearly Tamed: A Bear Claw Tale 3

Bearly Mated: A Bear Claw Tale 4

Also available in a boxed set:

The Complete Bear Claw Tales (Books 1-4)

Bound by Air: The Wardens of Terra Book 1

Star Kissed: A Wardens of Terra Short

Waterlocked: The Wardens of Terra Book 2

Moon Kissed: A Wardens of Terra Short

*Now in a boxed set and in audio!

The Maverick Pride Tales:

Purrfectly Mated: Paranormal Dating Agency: A Maverick Pride Tale 1

Purrfectly Kissed: Paranormal Dating Agency: A Maverick Pride Tale 2

Purrfectly Trapped: Paranormal Dating Agency: A Maverick Pride Tale 3

Purrfectly Caught: Paranormal Dating Agency: A Maverick Pride Tale 4

Purrfectly Naughty: Paranormal Dating Agency: A Maverick Pride Tale 5

Purrfectly Bound: Paranormal Dating Agency: A Maverick Pride Tale 6

Also available in 2 boxed sets:

The Maverick Pride Volume 1

The Maverick Pride Volume 2

Dire Wolf Mates:

Shake That Sass: Sassy Ever After: Dire Wolf Mates Book 1

Breaking Sass: Sassy Ever After: Dire Wolf Mates 2

Pinch of Sass: Sassy Ever After: Dire Wolf Mates 3

Also available in a boxed set:

Dire Wolf Mates Volume 1

Wyvern Protection Unit:

Trusting Her Protector

Tempting Her Protector

Tricking Her Protector

Standalones:

The Enforcer

Blood Song: A Sanguinem Council Book

EveL Worlds:

Chinchilla and the Devil: A FUCN'A BookSammi and the Jersey Bull: A FUCN'A Book

The Guardians of Chaos:

Wolf Shield: Guardians of Chaos Book 1

Dragon Shield: Guardians of Chaos Book 2

Stallion Shield: Guardians of Chaos Book 3

Panther Shield: Guardians of Chaos 4

Howl's Romance

Mated to the Werewolf Next Door: A Howl's Romance

The Tiger King's Christmas Bride

Claiming His Virgin Mate: Howls Romance

Check out these amazing anthologies where you can find some of my books

and the works of other awesome authors!

Coming Soon:

Ash: Speed Dating with the Denizens of Hell

Hungry Like Her Wolf: Magic and Mayhem Universe

Shifter Village: Hearts of Stone 3

Midnight Magic Anthology (Water Witch)

Mouse and the Ball: A FUCN'A Book

Tiger Claimed

For Fangs Sake

Tiger Denied

Werewolf Fever: A Macconwood Pack Novel 8

Moongate Island Captive

Witch Shield: Guardians of Chaos 5

Sweet As Candy (as seen in Once Upon An Ever After)

Taming Magic: The Angela Tanner Files 3

Rituals & Runes Anthology (Air Witch)

Excerpt from Code Wolf

"Are you fuckin' with me?"

"No, Randall, I assure you I am not fuckin' with you," Rafe Maccon eased his immense frame back into his oversized, black leather chair and narrowed his ice blue eyes at his Third and one of his oldest friends. How long had he known the man sitting in front of him?

Randall had come to Maccon City when Rafe was about ten, he looked the same then as he did now. Tall at six foot three inches, muscular, and more than a little intimidating to the Wolves under him with his long beard and equally long dark brown hair.

Rafe, however, was the Alpha. He was more amused than intimidated by his surly friend.

"A vacation?! What the fuck am I gonna do on a vacation? Come on, Rafe, this is bullshit!"

The door to Rafe's private office flew open and in strolled a very happy, very pregnant Charley Maccon, Rafe's wife. The Alpha's eyes glowed as they landed on his positively glowing mate. She wore a long, flowy dress. The shade was a pale-yellow color that, Randall admitted to himself, looked damn good with her creamy complexion and curly dark hair.

Their Alpha Female was quite something. There wasn't a Wolf Guard in the place who wouldn't lay down his/her life for her.

"Well, maybe you should consider a vacation to be a relaxing experience, Randy," she dropped a kiss on Randall's cheek and walked past him, over to her husband whom she kissed full on the mouth.

The way his Alpha's eyes homed in on her when she opened the door was nothing compared to the hungry gaze that followed her across the room.

Randall had noticed it took a while for Rafe to get used to his mate's habit of greeting everyone with a kiss or hug. Wolves were protective of their mates, but Randall thought his Alpha was doing an exceedingly good job of hiding his tension. Werewolves did not share very well.

Charley; however, had stood firm. That was the way she was raised, and she wasn't going to change for any, how had she put it? Neanderthal browbeating husband, regardless of how cute his ass was!

Randall had no direct knowledge if the "cute ass" statement was true or not. And he didn't want to know. He liked Charley though, had from the beginning. He was musically inclined and often took to one of the common rooms to strum his guitar or play a few keys on the piano.

Excerpt from Shifter Mountain
by C.D. Gorri

Keeton's Mountain Lion hissed angrily as he boarded the plane for the States. Three months on Moongate Island did nothing to repair his faith in people. Shifter or human, they pretty much sucked.

True, he was no longer being blackmailed by the sniveling cretin who'd been part of his last black ops assignment. Fucker had stepped on a landmine deep in the jungles of a place Keeton was not at liberty to name. Not even in his own head.

Fucking hell.

Yeah, it meant he could return home now, but to who? Keeton had no family waiting for him. His few friends were back on the island, but that was no place for his inner feline. The beast craved the hills and valleys of the New Jersey forests he called home.

He'd bought a hundred acres of forest off the beaten paths of New Jersey's Panther Mountains years ago. Even commissioned the building of a cabin deep in the woods. The design was environmentally conscientious and entirely sound. Two stories high, it had its own generators, additional solar paneling, and wind turbines for power, and indoor plumbing.

He wasn't an animal, for fuck's sake. But even if Keeton was going to avoid people, he didn't have to be uncomfortable doing it. Eyes closed, he sat seemingly at ease, but he was keeping tabs on every living thing around him on the plane.

Once a soldier, always a soldier, his two commanders, Callan McGregor and Landry Smyth, had said that often enough. Both men were Shifters, a unique Alpha and Omega pair who'd completed their Triad once they'd found their mate in Sage Freeman, a smart mouthed human female. That had been Keeton's cue to leave the island he'd called home for eighty-nine and a half days.

They hadn't kicked him out or anything. On the contrary. But he was restless and antsy. The island could no longer contain his need for isolation.

Memories of the disgust on Bruce Taylor's face when he'd seen Keeton lose control of his shift during a particularly bloody battle were forever ingrained in his brain. The human male had been a new recruit in the special ops task force where Keeton had served his country for the last five years in secret.

Dismantling dictatorships and stopping atrocities the likes of which he could hardly put a name to before they could ever see the light of day had been his job, and blackmail was his reward.

He'd kept the fact that he'd unwittingly told the secret about Shifters to the human from Callan and Landry until the night Bruce had died believing Keeton was the only one of his kind. The two men had investigated his claims, making sure that he never downloaded or emailed the proof he'd recorded with his phone the night Keeton lost control.

The half a million dollars he'd sent to Bruce's offshore bank was nothing. He didn't care about the money. It was simply the point of it all. The man had not trusted Keeton because of his dual nature. And he'd lost his life as a result.

"We need to stick to this route, Bruce," he growled at the human who'd become increasingly toxic to their two-man operation.

"Think I'm gonna trust a fucking animal. I'll go this way," the man argued.

After a few more minutes of trying to convince him, Keeton threw his hands up. His beast scratched at his skin, the animal sensing something was not right. The sounds of the explosion and Bruce's bitter cry rang in his ears, but he died before Keeton could ever hope to reach him.

It was his fault. He was the reason Bruce had died. After pledging his life to help save lives, he'd brought death instead.

Keeton was better off on his own.

Excerpt from Fangs For Nothin'
by C.D. Gorri

"Are you out of your mind?"

Xavier DuMont, Vampire and Prince of the Tenebris Clan out of DuMont, New Jersey, ran a hand over his face. It was almost five in the morning on Wednesday, and he was still going over the weekly requests and complaints.

He could not believe it. One after the other, he'd received dozens of requests for formal introductions for most of the eligible young females in the Clan by their parents or some family matchmaker or other. It was the 21st Century, and yet, the Vampires of the Tenebris Clan still thought he needed an arranged marriage to run things!

"No, Lucius, I assure you my mind is sound."

"How can you be thinking of going away? To some retreat? At this time of year! You know, the whole Clan is up in arms over the tax laws your father had set into motion before his demise. Some are questioning your right to rule. Then, there is still the matter of your mating—"

"Lucius, for the love of fuck! I know what is going on in my own Clan. I am even now revoking those tax laws, people will just have to be patient."

"And what about meeting with these young females? Maybe that will quell some of the unrest—"

"No! I am not inclined to take a mate at this time. My father's grave has barely begun to grow grass. There is no rush!"

"There is pressure though, sire," Lucius Redwing insisted.

He was Xavier's oldest and most reliable friend. At nearly three hundred years old, they'd known each other for a considerable length of time. Lucius had been his childhood companion when they'd fled France for the New World. After settling the town of DuMont, his father had not only been the most productive of the local normals, but he had taken over their branch of the Clan.

Breaking ties with the old regime, and establishing their own rule, the DuMonts had done exceedingly well. Of course, coming into the new century had been difficult for some, but Xavier was determined to do it, to breathe new life into the old-fashioned world of Vampires. He would see them succeed and blossom in this age that was simply exploding with technology.

"I know you have plans, sire. But the anxious mamas are already parading their daughters resumes as if they were applying for a job." Lucius grinned. He waved a manila envelope bursting with applications for audiences with him from the most prestigious Vampire families in all of DuMont.

"For fuck's sake, Luc. Get rid of them," Xavier growled, and ran a hand over his face.

"Now, now. Surely, you know enough not to disrespect tradition and courtesy. These families are your staunchest supporters. Without their aid, your ascension to leadership could be challenged. The right mate would stop all of that—"

"I will not be forced into this, Luc. If anyone wants to challenge me for the right to lead, then he or she can face me out in the open. Not hide behind some political game."

"But sire—"

"No. I will not be manipulated. You should know that of me, old friend."

"Yes. Of course." Lucius nodded, placing the hefty envelope on the corner of Xavier's desk.

Vampires did not always inherit the right to lead. Princes were not born but made. Wasn't that what his father had always said? And yet, royal blood flowed in his veins. And it was because of that blood *—his royal DuMont blood—*that so many hungry mamas yearned to tie one of their young to him for eternity.

Fortunately, Xavier had avoided them. He refused to be pressured to take any of the hungry misses for his mate, as of yet. But with his recent ascension, that pressure was now on full keel.

Shit and fuck.

"I've got an idea," Lucius said, thrusting a copy of *The Nightly News* at him.

"What is it, Luc? I am in no mood."

"Read there," his friend said, pointing at an article on the bottom left.

"A retreat? I haven't been on one of those since I was ninety."

"Yes, but remember the fun? I brought my *sheep* at the time, and you pouted because I wouldn't share her!"

"As I recall, she came quite willingly to my bed when summoned, Luc. Why do they still call them sheep? My gods, that is positively medieval!" he replied.

"In case normals see the newspaper, of course."

"Impossible. The Covens bespelled the paper to only go to supes."

"It has happened, Xavier. You know this as well as I."

"True. And Luc, I am sorry about Temple. That was your donor at the time, was it not?"

"Temple? Yes. Not to worry, sire. You always did woo the ladies without trying. Besides, now they have their own donors on hand. You do not need to bring one."

"You don't have to do that, you know."

"What?"

"Calling me sire."

"I do have to call you sire, *sire*. You are my Prince."

"Oh, do shut up. I am your friend, Luc. You've known me my entire life."

"Yes, sire."

"Luc," he growled his friend's name.

"Shall I make the arrangements then?"

"Fine. I will go to this retreat for the weekend if

only to shut you up. And to get away from all this."
He indicated the pile of correspondence.

"Very good, sire."

Excerpt from The Enforcer by C.D. Gorri

The moon would soon be full. Isabeau looked at the night sky and pulled the hood of her ivory sweater up over her fiery red curls. She passed between the red and sugar maples, a few tall beech trees, and a lonely pine when a low growl sounded next to her. She reached out to touch the thick fur of the adult she-Wolf who walked beside her through the forest trail.

"It's okay Artemis, let's finish our rounds and get home."

As she walked around the perimeter of her land she chanted an ancient language that few would be able to identify fortifying the wards around her large animal sanctuary. That was what the mortals around her thought it was, and for the most part they were correct.

To them, Isabeau Rose had just arrived in town a few years ago with the deed to five-hundred acres of Northern New Jersey farmland. Within a few months, she'd transformed the abandoned horse farm and the woods around it into a series of habitats for wild animals that were injured or discarded. Creatures that needed a haven for rehabilitation.

She had a main house for herself that boasted ten-bedrooms and six-full baths, an indoor pool and spa, two stables, one for her horses, the other for more exotic wildlife, two large red barns, and a state of the art veterinary clinic on the grounds.

"Out late, aren't you?" Beau turned around to find the source of the unfamiliar voice. She lifted her hand to calm Artemis who was ready to pounce on the intruder.

"Who are you?" she demanded.

"The real question is what are you doing out here so late? Surely your wards don't need reinforcement at this time of night, not out in this quiet New Jersey forest, Sorceress Rose?" The dark stranger spoke with an unearthly calm to his voice that put Beau on edge.

This was no mere mortal. She used her keen

sight to see him despite the darkness and almost gasped aloud. His face was perfect, except for a thin silver scar that ran from his left eyebrow to his chin. His eyes blazed cerulean blue fringed with impossibly dark lashes. They were carefully masked to hide his emotions.

About the Author

C.D. Gorri is a USA Today Bestselling author of steamy paranormal romance and urban fantasy. She is the creator of the Grazi Kelly Universe.

Join her mailing list here: https://www.cdgorri.com/newsletter

An avid reader with a profound love for books and literature, when she is not writing or taking care of her family, she can usually be found with a book or tablet in hand. C.D. lives in her home state of New Jersey where many of her characters or stories are based. Her tales are fast paced yet detailed with satisfying conclusions.

If you enjoy powerful heroines and loyal heroes who face relatable problems in supernatural settings, journey into the Grazi Kelly Universe today. You will find sassy, curvy heroines and sexy, love-driven heroes who find their HEAs between the pages. Werewolves, Bears, Dragons, Tigers, Witches, Romani, Lynxes, Foxes, Thunderbirds, Vampires, and many more Shifters and supernatural creatures dwell within her worlds. The most important thing is every mate in this universe is fated, loyal, and true lovers always get their happily ever afters.

Want to know how it all began? Enter the Grazi Kelly Universe with Wolf Moon: A Grazi Kelly Novel or pick up Charley's Christmas Wolf and dive into the Macconwood Pack Novel Series today.

For a complete list of C.D. Gorri's books visit her website here:

https://www.cdgorri.com/complete-book-list/

Thank you and happy reading!

del mare alla stella,
    C.D. Gorri

Follow C.D. Gorri here:
    http://www.cdgorri.com
    https://www.facebook.com/Cdgorribooks

https://www.bookbub.com/authors/c-d-gorri
https://twitter.com/cgor22
https://instagram.com/cdgorri/
https://www.goodreads.com/cdgorri
https://www.tiktok.com/@cdgorriauthor